GOOD BEHAVIOR

The Letty Dobesh Chronicles

OTHER TITLES BY
BLAKE CROUCH

GOOD BEHAVIOR

The Letty Dobesh Chronicles

BLAKE CROUCH

Published by Thomas & Mercer, Seattle

www.apub.com

Amazon, the Amazon logo, and Thomas & Mercer are trademarks of Amazon.com, Inc., or its affiliates.

ISBN-13: 9781503940499
ISBN-10: 1503940497

Cover design by Scott Barrie

Printed in the United States of America

For Michelle Dockery and
Juan Diego Botto

The bite of conscience, like the bite of a dog into a stone, is a stupidity. . . .

Can you give yourself your own evil and your own good and hang your own will over yourself as a law?

—Friedrich Nietzsche

CONTENTS

A NOTE FROM BLAKE CROUCH
ON *GOOD BEHAVIOR*

Letty Dobesh is hands-down the coolest thing creatively that has ever happened to me as a writer. Writing living, breathing people who are multidimensional and feel like someone you actually know is something I strive for; to me it has always been the hardest part of the job, and often I fall short of the goal. And if I do reach the goal, it's only after draft seven or eight of a novel—more an act of attrition than inspiration. A steady forming of the clay.

But the inception of Letty was a completely different and singular experience.

In March of 2009, I wasn't even thinking about Letty. I had become obsessed with a story idea, a sneakily simple premise: What if, during the course of your daily life, you accidentally got entangled in a contract killing? More specifically, what if you discovered that a contract killer were going to murder someone? Would you intervene? Try to stop it from happening? Go to the police? I tried to attack that idea a half dozen times but kept striking out. In all my failed attempts to write this story, my protagonist, the person who accidentally gets themselves involved in this mess, would simply go straight to the police, identify the contract killer, and save the target of the hit. End of story. And that didn't strike me as much fun. Kind of a one-note endeavor. The problem: all my protagonists were good people.

The first inklings of Letty occurred to me when I started asking myself what kind of character *wouldn't* or *couldn't* go straight to the police. I wondered, what if it were someone just out of prison on parole? Better yet, what if they were actually in the midst of a crime when they discovered this contract killer and his intentions? If that were the case, any attempt to go to the police would implicate them in their petty theft and send them back to prison. The story started to take shape, details beginning to fill themselves in. What if my antihero were robbing hotel rooms at a swanky resort when they overheard the details of this hit being discussed?

And with that question, a powerful image suddenly took hold of me. I saw a woman in a red wig, hiding in a closet with a duffel bag full of shit she'd spent the day stealing out of hotel rooms. I saw her staring through the slats of the sliding door, watching a man hire another man to kill his wife.

It still gives me chills when I think about it, because with that one image, I knew everything about this woman. Her spirit. Her fight. Her brokenness. Her struggles with addiction. I knew she had a son somewhere who she hadn't seen in years. I knew she'd been in and out of trouble her entire life. That she was currently living out of a cheap motel room, struggling every day not to use. Not to kill herself. I knew she was brilliant, inventive, charismatic, self-destructive, a chameleon. I knew she wasn't good or bad. She was authentic. Real. On a journey trying to discover who she really was, and wanting more than anything to make peace with that woman, even if she didn't fit inside the box society had drawn for her.

I loved Letty that moment. It wasn't like creating a character. It was like meeting a great friend for the first time. An instant creative connection. I just knew her.

Crouch watches the filming of episode 4, "Your Mama Had a Hard Night," surrounded by crew members.

In almost two decades of writing, the creation of Letty is one of the few moments of honest inspiration striking me like lightning out of a cloud. The only other moment that comes close is when I discovered the big mystery behind *Wayward Pines*.

I immediately got to work writing the first Letty Dobesh story, "The Pain of Others," which I submitted to *Alfred Hitchcock's Mystery Magazine*. Linda Landrigan, the editor at the magazine, chose to publish it in the March 2011 issue. And just like that, the rest of the world could know Letty, too.

I would go on to write two additional Letty novellas in the coming years; in between books in the *Wayward Pines* trilogy, her world was a great change of pace. Writing about her was fun—she always followed her gut and I never knew where she would take me.

Beginning in 2012, my life became busy with all things *Wayward Pines* (the books and the TV show), and I thought I'd seen the last of Letty for a while. But, true to her nature, Letty would not go quietly.

During the course of making *Wayward Pines* for FOX, I met a television writer and producer named Chad Hodge, who would become one of my best friends and a huge creative force in my life. Chad wrote the pilot script for *Wayward Pines*, created that show, and welcomed me into the process along the way. For context, our working relationship (TV writer and author) is generally unheard of in Hollywood, which typically tries to keep the writer of the source material as far removed from the process as possible.

Chad and I had such an amazing collaboration working on the first season of *Wayward Pines* that Chad started perusing the rest of my catalog for another potential project to work on. I told him I had these stories about this woman named Letty Dobesh. I warned him they weren't high-concept sci-fi thrillers like my *Wayward Pines* books. These were grounded in our world, and the concept was the character.

Chad read all the Letty stories and called me a few days later. The way he talked about Letty was the way I felt about her. He thought she was incredibly special and suggested we write a pilot script for this new show together.

When *Wayward Pines* filming wrapped, we began work on the pilot script of what would eventually become Letty's show, building the first episode primarily around "The Pain of Others," the story you're about to read. Chad came up with the title for the show, *Good Behavior*, and in April of 2015, we sold the pilot script and a pitch for a ten-episode season to Kevin Reilly at TNT, the same guy who had bought *Wayward Pines* from us when he ran FOX.

Just because you sell a TV show, it doesn't necessarily mean that show is destined to get made. More often than not, nothing ever happens. We knew that *Good Behavior* would live or die based on the casting of Letty, and here's where we got extremely lucky.

In the summer of 2015, *Downton Abbey*, one of the most iconic shows of the last decade, was in the process of wrapping up its final season. Which meant that one of its stars, Michelle Dockery (Lady Mary), was beginning to consider what her next acting role might be.

She read the script and loved Letty the same way Chad and I had.

Two months after that, on the strength of the pilot episode and three episode scripts written by Chad and me, TNT officially ordered *Good Behavior* to series.

So what exactly *is* this book?

First and foremost, it's the three stories I've written: "The Pain of Others," "Sunset Key," and "Grab." After each novella I have added some commentary about the work and the show, images, and other additional content from the journey I have taken with Letty. I like to think about it a little like a "choose your own adventure"—you can feel free to skip the additional content and come back another time, or never even look at it.

I hope this experiment turns out to be something more—a window into how an idea and a character evolve over time through different media.

I had the first notion of Letty in the spring of 2009 in some notebook scribbles. Over the next seven years, Letty went from an idea, to a story, to a script, to auditions, to table reads, to a cable-television show. Along the way, so many amazing people helped to make her the flawed, irresistible, broken, lovely, and brave character you're about to meet, and who you'll hopefully watch.

The best part of this experience is that Letty isn't just mine anymore. She belongs to my cocreator of *Good Behavior*, Chad Hodge. She belongs to Michelle Dockery, who delivers a devastating performance and takes Letty to places I could never have reached in a million years. She belongs to Charlotte Sieling, the director of the pilot episode, who set the "poetic noir" tone for the entire series. To Curt Beech, the production designer, Alonzo Wilson, the costume designer, and literally hundreds of people who worked long days and nights to help us make ten hours of television about a meth-addicted grifter who meets a contract killer and discovers that he may actually be her path to redemption.

This book isn't just three stories. It's the idea that a character doesn't only exist in prose. Letty is the amalgamation of prose and scripts and performances and finally, most importantly, the impression she leaves on you.

Thank you for reading.

Thank you for watching.

I hope you enjoy the ride.

Blake Crouch
Durango, Colorado
May 3, 2016

THE
PAIN OF
OTHERS

Letty Dobesh, five weeks out of a nine-month bit for felony theft at Fluvanna Correctional Center, straightened the red wig over her short auburn hair, adjusted the oversize Jimmy Choo sunglasses she'd lifted out of a locker two days ago at the Asheville Racquet Club, and handed a twenty-spot to the cabbie.

"Want change, miss?" he asked.

"On a $9.75 fare? What does your heart tell you?"

Past the bellhop and into the Grove Park Inn, carrying a small leather duffel bag, the cloudy autumn day just cool enough to warrant the fires at either end of the lobby, the fourteen-foot stone hearths sending forth intersecting drafts of warmth.

She sat down at a table on the outskirts of the lounge, noting the prickle in the tips of her ears that always started up right before. Adrenaline and fear and a shot of hope because you never knew what you might find. Better than sex on tweak.

The barkeep walked over and she ordered a San Pellegrino with lime. Checked her watch as he went back to the bar: 2:58 p.m. An older couple with glasses of wine cuddled on a sofa by the closest fireplace. A man in a navy blazer read a newspaper several tables away. Looked to her like money—top-shelf hair and skin. Must have owned a tanning bed or just returned from the Islands. Two men washed windows that overlooked the terrace. All in all, quiet for a Saturday afternoon, and she felt reasonably anonymous, though it didn't really matter. What would be recalled when the police showed up? An attractive thirty-something with curly red hair and ridiculous sunglasses.

As her watch beeped three o'clock, she picked out the sound of approaching footsteps—the barkeep returning with her Pellegrino. He set the sweating glass on the table and pulled a napkin out of his vest pocket.

She glanced up. Smiled. Good-looking kid. Compulsive weight lifter.

"What do I owe you?"

"On the house," he said.

She crushed the lime into the mineral water. Through the windows she could see the view from the terrace—bright trees under gray sky, downtown Asheville in the near distance, the crest of the Blue Ridge in the far, summits headless under the cloud deck. She sipped her drink and stared at the napkin the barkeep had left on the table. Four handwritten four-digit numbers. Took her thirty seconds to memorize them, and a quick look around confirmed what she had hoped—the window washers and the hotel guests remained locked and absorbed in their own worlds. She lifted the napkin and slid the keycard out from underneath it, across the glass tabletop and into her grasp. Then shredded the napkin, sprinkling the pieces into the hissing water.

2

One hour later, she fished her phone out of her purse as she stepped off the elevator and onto the fifth floor. The corridor plush and vacant. No housekeeping carts. An ice machine humming around the corner.

Down the north wing, Letty flushing with the satisfaction that came when things went pitch-perfect. She could have quit now and called it a great haul, her duffel bag sagging with the weight of three high-end laptops, $645 in cash, one phone, two tablets, and three fully raided minibars.

Standing in front of the closed door of 5212, she dialed the front desk on her stolen phone.

"Grove Park Inn. How may I direct your call?"

"Room 5212."

"Certainly."

Through the door, she heard the phone ringing, and she let it ring five times before ending the call and glancing up and down the corridor.

The master keycard unlocked the door.

5212 was the modest one of the four—a single king-size bed (unmade), tiled bathroom with a shower and garden tub, the mirror still beaded with condensation. In the sitting area, an armoire, a love seat, a leather chair, and floor-to-ceiling windows with a $350-a-night view of the Asheville skyline, the mountains, and a golf course—greens and fairways lined with pines and maple trees. A trace of expensive cologne lingered in the air, and the clothes on the bed smelled of cigar smoke.

She perused the bedside-table drawer, the armoire, the dresser, the drawers under the bathroom sink, the closet, the suitcase, even under the sofa cushions, which occasionally yielded big scores from the rich too cheap or lazy to use the hotel safe.

Room 5212 was a bust—nothing but three Romeo y Julieta cigars, which she of course pocketed—bonuses for the bellhop and barkeep.

On her way out, Letty unzipped her duffel bag and opened the minibar, her phone buzzing as she reached for a 1.5-ounce bottle of Glenlivet 12 Year.

Pressed "Talk."

"Yeah?"

"What room you in?"

"Fifty-two twelve."

"Get out of there. He's coming back."

She closed the minibar. "How long do I have?"

"I got tied up giving directions. You might not have any time."

She hoisted the duffel bag onto her shoulder, started toward the door, but the unmistakable sound of a keycard sliding into the slot stopped her cold.

A muffled voice: "I think you've got it upside down."

Letty opened the bifold closet doors and slipped in. With no doorknob on the inside, she had to pull them shut by the slats.

People entered the hotel suite. Letty let the duffel bag slide off her shoulder and onto the floor. Dug the phone out of her purse, powered it off as the door closed.

Through a ribbon of light, she watched two men walk past the closet, one in a navy blazer and khaki slacks, the other wearing a black suit, their faces obscured by the angle of the slats.

"Drink, Chase?"

"Jameson, if you've got it."

She heard the minibar open.

The man who wasn't named Chase poured the Irish whiskey into a rocks glass and cracked the cap on a bottle of beer, and the men settled themselves in the sitting area. Letty drew in deep breaths, her heart slamming in her chest, her knees soft, as if her legs might buckle at any moment.

"Chase, I need to hear you say you've really thought this through, that you're absolutely sure."

"I am. I only went to Victor when I realized there was no other way. I'm really in a bind."

"You brought the money?"

"Right here."

"Mind if I have a look?"

Letty heard locks unclasp, what might have been a briefcase opening.

"Now, you didn't just run down to your bank, ask for twenty-five large in hundred-dollar bills?"

"I went to Victor."

"Good. We're still thinking tomorrow, yes?"

"Tomorrow."

"I understand you have a son?"

"Skyler. He's seven. From a previous marriage."

"I want you to go out with your son tomorrow morning at ten. Buy some gas with a credit card. Go to Starbucks. Buy a coffee for yourself. A hot chocolate for Skyler. Wear a bright shirt. Flirt with the barista. Be memorable. Establish a record of you not being in your house from ten to noon."

"And then I just go home?"

"That's right."

"Can you tell me what you're going to do? So I can be prepared?"

"It'd be more natural—your conversations with the police, I mean—if you were truly surprised."

"I hear you on that, but I'll play it better if I know going in. It's the way I'd prefer it, Arnold."

"Where does your wife typically shower?"

"Upstairs in the master bath, right off our bedroom."

"As you're stepping out of the shower, is the toilet close?"

"Yeah, a few feet away."

"You're going to find her on the floor beside the toilet, neck broken like she'd slipped getting out of the shower. It happens all the time."

"Okay." Chase exhaled. "Okay, that'll work. I like that. Then I just call the police?"

"Call 911. Say you don't know if she's dead, but that she isn't moving."

"The police won't suspect I did this?"

"They may initially."

"I don't want that."

"Then don't have your wife killed. It's not a neat, easy transaction, and you shouldn't do business with anyone who tells you it is. The husband will always be suspected at first, but please understand I am very good at what I do. There will be an autopsy, but assuming you hold it together, it'll be ruled an accident. Now, what does your wife do for a living?"

"Not really anything now. She used to be a registered nurse. Why?"

"Just a little piece of information that helps me to prepare."

"That manila folder in the briefcase contains a recent photograph of Daphne. Address. House key. Floor plan. Everything you asked for. And I'll make sure the third window to the right of the front door is unlocked."

"I'll need your help distracting her while I'm getting inside. I want you to call her at precisely ten fifteen a.m. Tell her you can't find your wallet. You got a bedside table?"

"I do."

"You say you think you might have left it there, and would she please go check. That'll get her upstairs, give me time to get in."

"I should write this all down."

"No. Don't write anything down." The black-suited man rose to his feet. "I'm exhausted. I'm going to grab some shut-eye."

They came toward her, and Letty realized that Chase was the tanned and moneyed specimen she'd seen in the lobby.

"Once you walk out the door, Chase, there's no going back. You need to understand that."

She watched them shake hands, and then Arnold opened the door, saw Chase out, came back in, and closed and locked the door.

He went past the closet and sat down on the end of the bed. Pulled off his shoes and his black socks, and, as he sat there rubbing his feet, it occurred to Letty that he still wore his jacket, that he would want to hang it in the closet. Arnold stood and took off his jacket and started toward the closet.

The vibration of his phone stopped him. He pulled it out. Sighed.

"Yeah . . . No, it's fine." He unbuttoned his white oxford shirt.

Letty's hands trembled.

"The floral pattern, Jim." He laid his jacket across the dresser and turned his back to the closet. "Remember we talked about this?" His pants fell to his ankles, followed by his boxer shorts. He stepped out of them, climbed onto the bed, and lay on his back, his feet hanging off the end. "No, Jim. With the daffodils."

Already forty-five minutes late for work, Letty peered through the slats, saw Arnold's chest rising and falling, the man otherwise motionless and perfectly silent. She'd been standing in the same spot for almost ninety minutes, and, though she'd abandoned her heels, the closet didn't afford room, with the doors closed, for her to sit down or bend her knees to a sufficient degree of relief. Her legs had been cramping for the last half hour, hamstrings quivering.

She lifted her duffel bag, and as she pushed against the closet door, a rivulet of sweat ran down into the corner of her right eye. Blinking through the saltwater sting, she felt the door give, folding in upon itself with a subtle creak.

She stepped out into the room, glanced at the bed. Arnold hadn't moved.

At the door, she flipped back the inner lock, turned the handle as slowly as she could manage. The click of the retracting dead bolt sounded deafening. She eased the door back and stepped across the threshold.

She sat in the lobby, now noisy and crowded with the onset of cocktail hour. In her chair by the fireplace, she stared into the flames that roasted twelve-foot logs, the phone in her right hand, finger poised to press "Talk."

She couldn't make the call. She'd rehearsed it three times, but it didn't feel right. Hell, she didn't even know Daphne's last name or where the woman lived. Her story would require a leap of faith on the part of the investigating lawman, and when it came to credibility, she held a pair of twos. She couldn't use her real name, and meeting face-to-face with a detective could never happen. Letty had been convicted three times. Six years of cumulative incarceration. Her fourth felony offense, she'd be labeled a habitual criminal offender and entitled to commensurate sentencing guidelines at four times the max. She'd die in a federal prison.

So, seriously, all things considered, what did she care if some rich bitch got her ticket punched? If Letty hadn't hit room 5212 when she did, she'd already be at the diner, flirting for the big tips and still glowing from the afternoon's score. She tossed the phone back into her duffel. She should just leave. Pretend she'd never heard that conversation. She stole from people, innocent strangers, every chance she got. It never kept her up nights. Never put this torque in her gut. She'd get out of there, call in sick to work, buy two bottles of merlot, and head back to her miserable apartment. Maybe read a few chapters of that book she'd found at the thrift store—*Self-Defeating Behaviors: Free Yourself from the Habits, Compulsions, Feelings, and Attitudes That Hold You Back*. Pass out on the sofa again.

And you'll wake up tomorrow morning with a headache, a sour stomach, and a rotten taste in your mouth, and you'll look at yourself in that cracked mirror and hate what you see even more.

She cursed loud enough to attract the attention of an older man who'd dolled himself up for the evening, his eyes glaring at her over the top of the *Asheville Citizen-Times*. She slashed him with a sardonic smile and got up, enraged at herself over this swell of weakness. She took two steps. Everything changed. The anger melted. Exhilaration flooding in to take its place. In the emotion and fear of the moment, it had completely escaped her.

Room 5212 contained the manila folder with Daphne's photograph and address, but also a briefcase holding $25,000 in cash. Steal the money. Steal the folder. Save a life.

Even as she scrounged around her purse for the master keycard, she knew she wouldn't find it. In those first ten seconds of entry into Arnold's room, she'd set it on the dresser, where, she imagined, it still sat. She could feel the heat spreading through her face. The barkeep and the bellhop, her only contacts at the hotel, were already off shift. There'd be no replacement keycard.

She started through the lobby, wanting to run, punch through drywall, do something to expend the mounting rage.

She'd stopped to calm herself, leaning against one of the timber columns, her head swimming, when, thirty feet away, a bell rang, two brass doors spread apart, and the man named Arnold strode off the elevator, looking casual in blue jeans, cowboy boots, and a sports jacket. She followed his progress, watching him thread his way through the crowd and finally arrive at the entrance to the Sunset Terrace. He spoke with the hostess at the podium, and without even thinking about it, Letty found herself moving toward him, wishing she'd honed her pickpocket skills during one of her stints in prison. She'd known a woman at Fluvanna who had it down so cold she'd once lifted fifty wallets during a single day at Disney World. Arnold's back pockets were hidden under his navy jacket, no bulge visible, but people with sense didn't keep their wallets there. Inner pocket of his jacket, more likely, and she knew enough to know it took scary talent to snatch it from that location. You had to practically collide with the mark, your hands moving at light speed and with utter precision. She didn't have the chops.

Arnold stepped away from the hostess podium, and she watched him walk across the lobby into the Great Hall Bar, where he slid onto a barstool and waited to be served.

4

Letty cut in front of a striking couple and elbowed her way to the bar. The stool to Arnold's left sat unoccupied and she climbed onto it, let the duffel bag drop to her feet. She recognized the scent of his cologne, but she didn't look at him. Watched the barkeep instead, his back to her, mixing what appeared to be a Long Island Iced Tea, pouring shots from four different liquor bottles at once into a pint glass filled with ice.

Arnold drank from a long-necked bottle of Coors Light, picking at the label between sips. Something about his hands fascinated Letty, and she kept staring at them out of the corner of her eye.

When after two minutes the barkeep hadn't come over to take her drink order, she let slip an audible sigh, though in reality she sympathized. The lounge was crowded and she could tell the guy was doing the best he could.

She glanced over at Arnold, thinking he hadn't noticed her predicament. Like everyone else, exclusively engaged in his own world.

So it startled her when he spoke.

"Bartender."

And though the word hadn't been shouted, something in its tone implied a command that ought not be ignored. Clearly the barkeep picked up on it, too, because he was standing in front of Arnold almost instantaneously, like he'd been summoned.

"Get you another Coors?"

"Why don't you ask the lady what she wants?"

"Sorry, I didn't know she was with you."

"She's not. Still deserves a drink before the icecaps melt, don't you think?"

The barkeep emanated a distinct don't-fuck-with-me vibe that gave Letty the feeling he'd probably killed a number in medium security. A hardness in the eyes she recognized. But those eyes deferred to the customer seated to her right, flashing toward her with a kind of disbelief, like they'd grazed something harder than themselves and come away scratched.

"What would you like?"

"Grey Goose martini, little dirty, with a free-range olive."

"You got it."

Now or never. She turned toward Arnold, who'd already turned toward her. The tips of her ears on fire again, she got her first good look at him. Forty years old, she would have guessed. Smooth-shaven. Black hair, conservatively cropped. His collar just failing to hide the end of a tat, what might have been an erotic finger strangling his neck. Green eyes that exuded not so much hardness as an altogether otherworldly quality. She didn't know if it was Arnold's confidence or arrogance, but under different circumstances (and perhaps even these) she might have felt a strong attraction to the man.

"You're a lifesaver," she said.

He broke into a slight smile. "Do what I can."

She fell back on her break-into-in-case-of-emergency smile, the one that had disarmed a cop or two, that she'd used to talk her way out of a hotel room in Vegas.

"I'm Letty."

"Arnie."

She shook his hand.

"So's Letty short for—"

"Letisha. I know, it's awful."

"No, I like it. Nothing you hear every day."

The barkeep placed a martini in front of Letty, slid a fresh beer to Arnold.

"I got these," Letty said, going for her purse.

"Get out of here." Arnold reached into his jacket.

"Actually," the barkeep said, "these are on me. Sorry about the wait, guys."

Letty raised her martini by the stem, clinked her glass against the neck of Arnie's bottle.

"Cheers."

"New friends."

They drank.

"So where you from?" Arnie asked.

"Recently moved here."

"Nice town."

"S'okay."

She could already feel the conversation beginning to strain, climbing toward a stall.

"I have a confession to make," she said.

"What's that?"

"I shouldn't. You'll think I'm awful."

"I already think you're awful. Go for it." He bumped his shoulder against hers as he said it, and she loved the contact.

"I'm here for a blind date."

"What'd you do? Ditch the guy?"

"No, I'm chickening out. I don't want to go through with it."

"You were supposed to meet him in the lobby?"

"This bar. I got scared. Saw you sitting here. I'm a bad person, I know."

Arnold laughed and slugged back the dregs of his first beer. "How do you know I'm not the guy?"

"Oh God, are you?"

He raised his eyebrows as if dragging out the suspense.

Finally said, "No, but this poor sap's probably walking around trying to find you. He know what you look like?"

"General description."

"So you want to hide out with me. Is that it?"

She dusted off her cute, pouty face. "If it's not too much trouble. I can't promise to be witty and engaging, but I will get the next round." She sipped her drink, staring him down over the lip of the martini glass, the salt of the olive juice and the vodka burn flaring on the sides of her tongue.

"Do you one better," he said.

"How's that?"

"Well, if we're really going to sell the thing, totally throw this guy off your trail, you should probably have dinner with me."

5

They told each other lies over a beautiful meal, Letty becoming a high-school English teacher and aspiring novelist. She would rise at four every morning and write for three hours before driving into work, the book already five hundred pages, single-spaced, about a man who bears a strong likeness to a movie star and uses that resemblance to storm the Broadway scene and ultimately Hollywood, to comic and tragic ends.

Arnold worked for a philanthropist based out of Tampa, Florida. Had come to Asheville to investigate and interview the CEO of a research-and-development think tank that had applied for funding.

"What exactly are they involved in?" Letty asked after the waiter had set down her steak and topped off her wineglass, and she'd sliced into the meat, savoring both the perfection of her medium-rare porterhouse and the impromptu train of bullshit Arnold rattled off about bioinformatics and cancer applications.

They killed two bottles of a great bordeaux, split a chocolate lava cake, and wrapped things up with a pair of cognacs, sharing a couch by a fireplace in the lobby, Letty adding up the three martinis, her share of the wine (more than a bottle), and now this Rémy Martin, which was going down way too easy. Part of her sounding the alarm—*You're letting it get away from you.* The rest wondering how fast the bellhop pulling a cart of luggage toward the elevators could score her some tweak and would Arnold be down for it if he did?

◈

In the dull brass doors, she watched her and Arnold's warped reflection. He kissed the back of her neck, those fascinating hands around her waist, which she was too drunk to bother sucking in.

They stumbled out onto the fifth floor, and by the time she realized her mistake, there was nothing to be done, having instinctively turned down the north wing toward room 5212, as if she'd been up there before.

◈

"I have another confession to make," Letty said while Arnold rummaged through the minibar.

"What's that?"

"I'm not a redhead."

He glanced over the top of the open door as Letty tugged off her wig.

"You look upset," she said.

He stood up, kicked the door closed with the tip of his boot, and set the bottles of beer on the dresser beside the keycard Letty had left behind four hours ago.

Sauntered toward her in slow, measured steps, stopping less than an inch away, his belt buckle grazing her navel.

"Are you upset?" she slurred.

He ran his fingers through her short auburn hair to the base of her neck. She thought she felt his hands tightening around her throat, her carotid artery pulsing against the pressure. Looked up. Green eyes. Suspicion. Lust. She swayed in her heels. He ran his hands down her waist, over the curve of her hips, moved his right hand onto the small of her back and pulled her against him.

Music bled through from the next room, something midtempo and synthesized from the '80s—Air Supply or worse.

They kept dancing after the music had stopped, a mutual drunken stagger, Arnold working them back toward the wall, where his hand fumbled for the light dimmer.

◈

She woke in the middle of the night with a violent thirst, and, even lying on a pillow, it felt like someone had caved her skull in while she slept, the red digits of the alarm clock continually descending into place like the endless motion of a barbershop pole. The bulk of a man snored beside her, his rank breath warming the back of her neck. She lay naked with a cover twisted between her legs. Couldn't recall passing out. The events after returning to this room lay in shards of memory—slamming shots of Absolut out of tiny bottles. A fast, hard fuck that didn't approach the hype. She wondered if she'd said anything to undermine the evening's lies, and just the threat of it, considering the man whose bed she shared, broke a cold sweat across her forehead. She shut her eyes. Heard her father's voice—all cigarette growl and whiskey-tongued—which whispered to her on nights like these, lying in the beds of strange men and the darkness spinning, or in a lonely cell, cursing her back to sleep. Words that, deep in her heart, she knew were true.

6

Threads of light stole in around the blinds.

9:12 a.m.

A line of painful brilliance underscored the bathroom door, the shower rushing on the other side. She sat up in bed and threw back the covers and brought her palms to her temples, pressing against the vibrant ache.

Out of bed, onto her feet, listing and nauseated. Stepped into her cashmere tank dress and pulled the straps over her shoulders. Last time she'd seen that leather briefcase full of money, it had been sitting on the floor beside the love seat, but it had since been moved. She got down on her hands and knees and peered under the couch, then under the bed.

Nothing.

As she opened the closet, Arnold yelled from the shower, "Letty, you up?"

The briefcase leaned against the wall on the top shelf inside the closet, and she had to rise on the balls of her feet to grasp it.

"Letty!"

Pulled the briefcase down, walked over to the bathroom door.

"Yeah, I'm up," she said.

"How do you feel?"

"Like death."

She squatted down, fingering the clasps on the briefcase.

"I didn't mention it last night," he said, "but I've got this meeting to go to."

"This morning?"

"Unfortunately."

"Is this with the think tank?"

"Yeah, exactly."

Her thumbs depressed two buttons. The clasps released.

"I wanted to have breakfast with you," she said and opened the case.

"We could do dinner."

Twenty-five thousand in cash didn't look all that impressive—just five slim packets of hundos.

"You staying here tonight?" she asked, lifting one, flipping through the crisp, clean bills, breathing in the ink and the paper.

"I would," he said, "if you wanted to get together again."

The shower cut off. She heard the curtain whisk back. Tossed the packet into the briefcase, grabbed the manila folder, leafed through the contents: floor plan, house key, one page of typewritten notes, and a black-and-white photograph of a woman who couldn't have been more than a year or two past thirty. The shot was candid, or trying to be, Daphne in the foreground, in startling focus, surrounded by clusters of blurry rhododendrons. Her hair long, black, straight. Skin preternaturally pale. A remote and icy beauty.

Arnold was toweling off now.

"We could definitely meet for dinner tonight," Letty said as she scanned the address on the page of notes: 712 Hamlet Court.

The tiny motor of an electric razor started up. She closed the briefcase. Her heels lay toppled on the carpet at the foot of the bed, and she stepped into them, slung her duffel bag onto her shoulder.

"Maybe we could grab dinner downtown," Arnold said over the whine of his razor. "I'd like to see more of Asheville."

"Absolutely," she said, lifting the briefcase. "I'll take you barhopping. I know a few good ones. We'll hit the Westville Pub. Great beer bar."

"Now you're talking."

Twelve feet to the door. To being done with all of this. Her biggest score.

She turned back the inner lock, reached down for the handle.

Arnold said something from the bathroom that she missed. She saw herself slipping out into the corridor, heard the soft click of the door shutting behind her. Felt the tension of waiting for the elevator.

Letty turned back from the door, returned the briefcase to the closet shelf. Hardest thing she'd ever done.

She set her bag down and knocked on the bathroom door. "Can I come in, Arnie?"

"Yeah."

He turned off the razor as she opened the door, frowned when he saw her. Steam rising off his shoulders. "You're dressed."

"I want to go back to my apartment, get a shower there."

"You can stay here while I go to my meeting."

"I need to let my dog out, get some papers graded. I'll leave my number on the bedside table."

He stepped away from the sink, embraced her, the towel damp around his waist, said, "I can't wait to see you tonight."

And she kissed him like she meant it.

Letty ran through the lobby, past the front desk, out into a cool fall morning. She forced a twenty into the bellhop's hand, and he relinquished the car service he'd called for another guest.

"You know Hamlet Court?" she asked when the bellhop had shut her into the backseat of the Lincoln Town Car.

The driver glanced back, a light-skinned Haitian with blue eyes. "I will find. You have street number?"

"Seven twelve." As he punched the address into the GPS unit, Letty handed a hundred-dollar bill into the front seat. "I'm sorry, but I need you to speed."

❖

Through the streets of the old southern city, the downtown architecture catching early light—city hall, the Vance Monument, the Basilica of Saint Lawrence, where a few churchgoers straggled in for morning mass—and, on the outskirts of Letty's perception, secondary to her inner frenzy, a spectrum of Appalachian color: copper hillsides, spotless blue, the Black Mountain summits enameled with rime ice. A classic autumn day in the Swannanoa Valley.

They turned onto an oak-lined boulevard, red and gold leaves plastered to the pavement.

"We're going into Montford?" Letty asked.

"That's what the computer says to me."

Hamlet Court was a secluded dead end off the B-and-B bustle of Montford Avenue, approximately a half mile long, and home to a dozen Victorian mansions.

The entrance to 712 stood at the end of the cul-de-sac, through a brick archway just spacious enough to accommodate a single car.

"Stop the car," Letty said.

"I take you all the way up."

"I don't want you to take me all the way."

She climbed out of the car at 10:04. Hurried to the end of the street and under the archway, glancing at the name on a large black mailbox: Rochefort.

The residence sat toward the back of the property, which sloped up across a masterfully landscaped yard shaded with maple and spruce trees, dotted with stone sculptures—fountains, birdbaths, angels—and not a leaf to be seen on the pockets of lush green grass.

An engine turned over near the house. Letty stepped off the drive and crawled into a thicket of mountain laurel as a boxy Mercedes G-Class rolled past. Through the branches and tinted glass, she glimpsed Chase at the wheel, a young boy in a booster in the backseat. The car ride over had only intensified her nausea, and as the diesel engine faded away, she put her finger down her throat and retched in the leaves.

She felt instantly better. Weaker. Less drunk. But better.

Only when the Mercedes had disappeared did she climb out of the bushes. Shivering, shoulders scraped, head pounding with not only a hangover, but a new element of suffering—coffee deprivation.

She jogged uphill to where the driveway widened and cut a roomy circle back into itself. Up the brick steps onto the covered porch, where she rang the doorbell twice, struggling to catch her breath.

10:08 by her phone as footsteps approached from the other side of the door.

When it finally opened and Daphne Rochefort stood on the threshold in a lavender terry-cloth robe, Letty realized she had given no prior consideration to exactly what she might say to this woman, had thought through and executed getting here but nothing after.

"Yes?"

"Daphne?"

The woman's eyes narrowed. "What can I do for you?" Though at face value the words were all southern hospitality, the delivery carried a distinct northern draft.

Letty rubbed her bare arms, figured she probably still reeked of alcohol and vomit.

"There's a man coming here to kill you."

"Pardon?"

"I know this must sound—"

"You smell like booze."

"You have to listen to me."

"I want you off my porch."

"Please, just—"

"I'm calling the police."

"Good, call the police."

Daphne retreated to slam the door, but Letty darted forward, planting her right heel across the doorframe. "I'm trying to help you. Just give me two minutes."

Letty followed Daphne past the staircase, down a hallway, and into an enormous kitchen full of marble and stainless steel, redolent of chopped onions and cooking eggs. Daphne went to the stove, flipped an omelet, and began to peel a banana. "What's your name?"

"It's not important."

"So talk," she said.

Letty stood across the island from her, light flooding in through the large windows behind the sink, the coffeemaker at the end of its brewing cycle, gurgling like it'd had its throat cut.

"Here's the CliffsNotes," Letty said, "because we don't have much time. I went to the Grove Park Inn yesterday. Someone hooked me up with a master keycard, tipped me off to which rooms might be worth hitting."

"You're a thief."

"I was in the last room of the day when the guest came back unexpectedly. I had to hide in the closet."

"I'm failing to see—"

"Chase was with him." Daphne stopped slicing the banana. "Your husband gave this man, Arnold, a key to your house. A photo of you. A floor plan. And twenty-five thousand dollars to murder you."

Daphne looked up from the cutting board, her bright black eyes leveled upon Letty like a double-barreled shotgun. Her smile exposed a row of exquisite teeth.

"I want you to leave right now."

"You think I'm lying? I didn't *want* to come here. I had a chance to steal the twenty-five thousand this morning. Could've gone home, had nothing more to do with any of this. You don't know me, but this isn't like me, this . . . selflessness. I've been to prison too many times. I can't take another felony charge. Getting involved in this was a great risk for me."

Daphne took up the knife again, continued cutting the banana.

Letty spotted the clock on the microwave. "I can prove it to you. It's 10:11. In exactly four minutes, your husband will call you. He'll tell you he can't find his wallet. He'll ask you to go upstairs to your bedroom and check in his bedside table. If he calls, will you believe me?"

Daphne glanced at the microwave clock, then back at Letty. Honest-to-God fear in her eyes for the first time. A solemn, crushing focus. She nodded. The eggs burning.

"How will he reach you?" Letty asked. "Landline? Cell?"

"My iPhone."

"Can we take the Beamer in the driveway?"

"I'm not leaving with you."

"You don't understand. By the time your husband calls you, it'll be too late. The point of the phone call is to get you upstairs so Arnold can break in."

"You want to leave right now?"

"This second."

Daphne moved the pan to a cold burner and turned off the gas. They walked back down the hall, past a wall adorned with family and individual portraits and a collage of photographs—grinning babies and toddlers.

In the foyer, Daphne plucked a set of keys from a ceramic bowl beside a coatrack and opened the front door. The yard brilliant with strands of light that passed through the trees and struck the lawn in splashes of green.

Ten steps from the silver Beamer, Letty grabbed Daphne's arm and spun her around with a hard jerk.

"Ouch."

"Back inside."

"Why?"

"There's a car parked halfway up your driveway behind the rhododendron."

They went back up the steps.

"You have the house key?" Letty asked.

They crossed the porch, Daphne struggling with the keys as they arrived at the door, finally sliding the right one into the dead bolt. Back into the house and Daphne shut the wide oak door after them, relocked the dead bolt, the doorknob, the chain.

"I should check the back door," Daphne said.

"It doesn't matter. He has a key and Chase left a window open. You have a gun in the house?"

Daphne nodded.

"Show me."

Daphne ran up the staircase, Letty kicking off her heels as she followed. By the top of the stairs, her pulse had become a thumping in her temples—exertion and panic. They turned down a hallway, passed an office, a bright-white studio filled with sunlight and tedious acrylic paintings of mountain scenes, then two children's bedrooms that emanated the frozen perfection of unlived-in space. At the end of the hall, French doors opened into a master suite built in the shape of an octagon, the walls rising to a vaulted ceiling that was punctured with skylights.

Chirping crickets stopped them both. Daphne withdrew her iPhone from the pocket of her robe and forced a smile that managed to bleed through into her voice.

"Hi, honey . . . No, it's fine . . . Upstairs . . . Sure." Daphne stepped into a walk-in closet, hit the lights. Letty lingered in the doorway, watched her reach through a wall of suits and emerge a moment later with a pump-action shotgun.

She mouthed, "Loaded?"

Daphne nodded. "Chase, it's not in here. Want me to check downstairs?" Letty took the gun from Daphne. "All right," Daphne said. "You two have fun."

Letty whispered, "Call 911," and while Daphne dialed, Letty flicked off the safety and racked a shell into the chamber. She peered around the corner, down the hall. The house stood silent. She moved out of the closet and into a lavish master bath the size of her apartment, the tile cool on her bare feet.

Garden tub. Immense stone shower with a chrome fixture a foot in diameter. Long countertops cut from Italian granite.

Letty opened the glass shower door and cranked the handle. Preheated water rained down. The glass steamed. She returned to the bedroom, shutting the door behind her, found Daphne standing just inside the closet.

"Why'd you run the shower?" she whispered.

"Are the police coming?"

"Yes."

Letty killed the lights. "Go crouch down in the corner behind those dresses and turn your phone off." As Daphne retreated into the darkness, Letty pulled the door closed and padded out into the hall, making her way between the easels in the studio to the big windows that overlooked the front yard.

The car in the driveway hadn't moved. A black 4Runner. Empty.

She walked out into the hall, straining to pick out the whine of approaching sirens.

Had the central heat been running, it would've completely escaped her notice, and even in the perfect silence she still nearly missed it—just around the corner and several feet down, the faintest groan of hardwood fibers bowing under the weight of a footstep.

Letty backpedaled into the studio and stepped behind the open door.

Through the crack, she eyed the hall.

Arnold appeared without a sound, wearing blue jeans and a fleece pullover. For a second, she thought there must be something wrong with his hands, their paleness. Latex gloves. Navy socks with strips of rubber gripping kept his footfalls absolutely silent, and he moved slowly and with great precision down the hall, a black pistol at his side that had been fitted with a long suppressor.

Arnold stopped in the doorway of the master suite.

Waited a full minute.

Nothing but the white noise of the shower.

In the time it took Letty to step out from behind the door and peek into the hall, Arnold had disappeared.

She held the shotgun at waist level and started toward the master suite. The half-speed fog of her hangover was replaced with a throbbing vigilance and a metal taste in the back of her throat that had come only a handful of times in her life—fights in prison, the three occasions she'd faced a judge to be sentenced, her father's funeral.

She entered the master suite again. Steam poured out of the bathroom and Arnold stood in the doorway with his back to her. She felt light-headed and weak, unable to summon her voice just yet, not fully committed to the idea of being in this moment.

Arnold walked into the steamy bathroom and Letty edged farther into the room, past the unmade bed and the stair-climber, the shotgun trained on Arnold's back through the open doorway, slightly obscured in the mist.

"You have a shotgun pointed at your back."

He flinched at the sound of her voice. "Don't turn around. Don't move. Drop the gun." Arnold didn't move, but he didn't drop the gun either. "Don't make the mistake of thinking I'll tell you again." It clattered on the tile. "Kick it away from you." The gun slid across the floor, coming to rest against the cabinets under the sink. Letty closed the distance between them, now standing in the bathroom doorway, close enough to smell the remnants of his cologne. "Keep your hands out in front of you and turn around." When he saw her, his eyes betrayed only a glimmer of surprise. "Sit down, Arnold." He sat at the base of the shower as Letty stepped into the bathroom, clouds of mist swirling between them.

He said, "What are you, a cop?"

"I was in your room yesterday afternoon when you and Chase came in. I hid in the closet. Heard everything you said."

"So you're a thief. That means we can work this out."

"How's that?"

"Can I get something out of my pocket?"

"Slowly."

He reached into his fleece jacket, withdrew a set of keys, let them jingle. "The 4Runner's new. There's a briefcase with twenty-five thousand in cash in the front seat."

"I know about the briefcase."

"I can just go home. That's a good score for you, Letty. Bet you never had a payday like that."

"And you go back to doing what you do?"

He smiled, shook his head. "The people I work for . . . if they want someone dead, that person's going to die. It's *their* will that causes it to happen. Not mine. They pull the trigger. I'm just the bullet. The damage. And I'm not the only bullet. So really, Letty. Why get yourself tangled up in this? You're a thief, a tweaker. You been to prison?"

"Yeah."

"So why not stay out of the affairs of the spoiled rich? Why do you care so much to interfere? To put yourself at risk, which you've done?"

"Late at night, when you're alone, do you ever feel like somewhere along the way, you crossed this line you didn't see? Actually sold *yourself* out?"

Arnold just stared at her as the shower beat down on the stone.

"I thought I was completely lost, Arnie. And then I found myself hiding in that closet in your room, and I saw a chance to go back to the other side of the line."

Letty heard the closet door swing open. Daphne came and stood beside her.

"My husband paid you to kill me?"

Arnold made no response. Daphne walked over to the sinks, bent down, picked up his gun.

"You shouldn't touch that, Daphne. The police are coming."

"Not yet they aren't."

"What are you talking about?"

"You're an ex-con. I don't want you taking any flak, considering you were stealing from the guests of the Grove Park Inn when you got involved. Take his car and his money. I'll call the police after you're gone."

"That's your money, Daphne."

"No, it's Chase's." She aimed Arnold's gun at him. "Keys."

He tossed them to Letty.

"I don't want to leave you here alone with him, Daphne."

"I'll be all right." She took the shotgun.

"I'm not leaving you."

"You saved my life, Letty. I'll never forget it. Now go."

8

Five days later, at 6:01 p.m., Chase Rochefort stepped off the elevator, dressed to the nines in a light-gray Coppley and a cobalt oxford, engaged with his iPhone as he breezed through the lobby of the neo-Gothic Jackson Building, whose twelfth floor housed his law practice—Rochefort, Bloodsworth & Sax, LLC. The stunning redhead followed him out onto the street, sprouting her umbrella against the drizzly Friday evening. Trailed him along South Pack Square to North Market, and then several blocks to the intersection with Woodfin, where Rochefort entered the Sheraton Hotel.

He sat at the corner of the chophouse bar, letting his Chilean sea bass turn cold and drinking double Powers on the rocks with twists of lemon like his life depended on it. Halfway through his sixth, the barstool beside him opened up and Letty claimed it and ordered a glass of merlot.

While the barkeep poured her wine, Letty reached over, patted Chase's hand, and asked with faux empathy, "How you holding up?" Searched his face for some tell of the preceding week's stress, but no indication presented aside from a darkness under his eyes that had mostly been erased with concealer and the blush of Irish whiskey.

He worked up a glassy-eyed smile, slurred, "We know each other?"

"Well, I certainly know you."

The barkeep returned with her wine. "That's ten dollars. Would you like to start a—"

Chase tapped his chest. "My tab."

"Of course, Mr. Rochefort."

Chase banged his rocks glass against Letty's wineglass and threw back the rest of his whiskey. "Have I sued you before?" he asked, excavating the lemon from the melting cubes of ice, crunching the rind between his back molars.

"No, you haven't sued me."

"Good." He grinned. "I've sued half the people in this town."

The barkeep arrived with a fresh double Powers on the rocks and swapped it out for Chase's empty glass.

"But I was curious about something," Letty asked, letting her left knee brush against his leg.

"What's that?"

"I've read the *Citizen-Times* cover to cover for the last five days and there's been no mention of it." He sipped his new drink, Letty wondering about the depth of his intoxication, how much of this was sliding past him. "I've called your home. Never got an answer. You and Skyler have been living out of this hotel all week, and you come down here and drink yourself into a stupor every night."

His face paled slightly through the Powers glow. "Who are you?"

"I was there, Chase."

"Where? What are you talking about?"

She leaned over, whispered in his ear: "Room 5212 at the Grove Park Inn when you met with Arnold LeBreck and hired him to murder your wife. I was in the closet. I heard everything."

He drew back, the noise of the chophouse swelling—thirty separate conversations intermingled with the clink of glassware and china.

She said, "Last Sunday morning, I went to your house in Montford. I told your wife everything—"

"Oh Jesus."

"—and when I left, she was holding a shotgun on Mr. LeBreck and on the verge of calling the police. I should never have left her . . .

"But as I just mentioned, nothing in the papers. No sign of Daphne. So I'm sitting here wondering what happened, but before you answer, let me tell you that I've written a letter to the Asheville Police Department providing a firsthand account, and it will be delivered tomorrow by a friend of mine should I become scarce."

This last part was a lie. She'd only just thought of it.

Chase drained his whiskey in one shot and slammed the glass down on the bar.

"Why won't you go back to your house, Chase? What did you do there on Sunday morning after I left? What did you do to your wife?"

Chase grabbed the side of the bar to steady his hands. He closed his eyes, opened them again. The barkeep set another Powers in front of him and took away his cold, untouched dinner plate.

"You have no idea what you've done," he said.

"I'm going back to your house," Letty said. "Tonight. Am I going to find her dead? Why won't you tell me, instead of sitting here in denial, pretending none of this has happened?"

Chase stared down the length of the bar for a full minute, then rubbed his palms into his eyes, smearing a bit of eyeliner.

Another greedy sip of Powers and he said, "I met Daphne after my first wife died. Skyler was two, and my parents kept him for a week, made me take a trip. We met in Oranjestad. You know Aruba? She could be so engaging when she wanted to be.

"We'd been married a year when I caught the first glimpse of what she really was. Friend of ours had gotten divorced and Daphne was consoling her on the telephone. It was a small thing, but I suddenly realized what she was doing. My wife had this way of talking to you so you'd think she was comforting you when she was actually salting your wounds. I saw her do it again and again. Even with me. With my son. It was like the pain of others attracted her. Filled her up with this black joy. Please," he slurred. "Don't go back there. Just leave it alone."

"So it turns out your wife's a bitch after all, and you want her dead. That's so original." Letty had a strong desire to take the Beretta 84 pistol out of her purse and jam it into Chase's ribs, make him come along with her, rub his face in whatever he'd done. Instead, she climbed down from the barstool, said, "Have a wonderful night of freedom, Chase. It may be your last."

9

Letty parked her 4Runner in the cul-de-sac and walked up the driveway toward the Rochefort residence. The rain had further dissolved into a cold, fine mist, and all she could see of the Victorian was the lamplight that pushed through a row of tall, arched windows on the second floor. At the front door, she peered through a panel of stained glass, saw a sliver of the low-lit hallway—empty.

She knocked on the door and waited, but no one came.

She slid the third window open. She lifted the shade, saw the living room illuminated by a sole piano lamp on the baby grand. Climbed over the back of the upholstered sofa and closed the window behind her.

"Daphne?"

The hardwood groaned under her footsteps as she moved through the living room and up the stairs. The bed in the master suite looked slept in, covers thrown back, sheets wrinkled, clothes hanging off the sides.

Letty went downstairs into the kitchen and, as she stared into a sinkful of dirty dishes, noticed the music—some soothing adagio—drifting up from a remote corner of the house.

She walked around the island to a closed door near the breakfast nook.

Opened it. The music strengthening.

Steps descended into a subterranean level of the residence, and she followed them down until she reached a checkerboard floor made of limestone composite. To the left, a washing machine and dryer stood in the utility alcove surrounded by hampers of unwashed laundry that reeked of mildew.

Letty went right, the music getting louder.

Rounded a corner and stopped.

The brick room was twenty feet by twenty and lined with metal wine racks, the top rows of bottles glazed with dust.

Beside an easel lay a Bose CD player, a set of Wüsthof kitchen knives, and boxes of gauze and bandages. Hanging from the ceiling of the wine cellar by a chain under her arms—Letty's eyes welled up—Daphne.

Then the lifeless body shifted and released a baritone wail.

This wasn't Daphne.

Letty recognized the tattoo of the strangling hands as Arnold LeBreck painfully lifted his head and fixed his eyes upon Letty, and then something behind her.

Letty's stomach fell.

She spun around.

Daphne stood five feet away, wearing a black rubber apron streaked with paint or blood and a white surgical mask, her black hair pinned up except for a few loose strands that splayed across her shoulders.

She pointed a shotgun at Letty's face, and something in that black hole suggested the flawed philosophical underpinnings that had landed Letty in this moment. No more hating herself, no avoiding the mirror, letting her father whisper her to sleep, no books on learning to love yourself or striving to become something her DNA could not support. She was facing down a shotgun, on the verge of an awful death, not because she was an evil person, but because she wasn't evil enough.

Letty thought fast. "Oh, thank God. You're not hurt."

Daphne said through the mask, "What are you doing here?"

"Making sure you're okay. I ran into Chase—"

"What'd he tell you? I warned him to let me have a week with Arnold, and then I'd be out of his life."

"He didn't tell me anything, Daphne. That's why I came over. To check on you."

Arnold moaned and twitched, managed to get himself swinging back and forth over the wide drain in the floor like a pendulum.

"That man was going to kill me," Daphne said.

"I know, honey. I saved you. Remember?" The smell was staggering, Letty's eyes beginning to water, her stomach to churn. "Well, I see you're okay, so I'll slip out, let you—"

"You shouldn't have come back."

"I didn't see anything in the papers about your husband or Arnold. I thought something had happened to you after I left last Sunday."

Daphne just stared at her. The face mask sucking in and out. At last she said, "You think what I'm doing is—"

"No, no, no. I'm not here to . . . That man was going to kill you. He deserves whatever happens to him. Think of all the other people he's murdered for money."

"You saw my painting?"

"Um, yeah."

"What do you think?"

"What do *I* think?"

"Do you like it?"

"Oh, yes. It's . . . thought-provoking and—"

"Some parts of Arnold's portrait are actually painted with Arnold."

Daphne's arms sagged with the weight of the shotgun, the barrel now aligned with Letty's throat.

"I saved your life," Letty said.

"And I meant what I said. I won't ever forget it. Now go on into the wine cellar. Just push Arnold back and stand over the drain."

"Daphne—"

"*You'd* be a lovely subject."

Letty's right hand grazed the zipper of her all-time favorite score—a Chanel quilted-leather handbag she'd stolen out of the Grand Hyatt in New York City. Thirty-five hundred at Saks Fifth Avenue.

"Get your hand away from there."

"My phone's vibrating."

"Give it to me."

Letty unzipped the bag, pulled out the phone with her left hand, let her right slip inside. Any number of ways to fumble in front of a gaping shotgun barrel.

She said, "Here," tossed the phone to Daphne, and as the device arced through the air, Letty's right hand grasped the Beretta and thumbed off the safety.

She squeezed the trigger as Daphne caught the phone.

The shotgun blasted into the ceiling, shards of blond brick raining down and Daphne stumbling back into the wall as blood ran in a thin black line out of a hole in her throat.

Letty pulled out the pistol—no sense in doing further damage to her handbag—and shot her three times in the chest.

The shotgun and the phone hit the limestone, and Daphne slid down into a sitting position against the wall. Out from under her rubber apron, blood expanded through little impulse ripples whose wavelengths increased with the fading pump of her heart. Within ten seconds, she'd lost the strength or will to clutch her throat, her eyes already beginning to empty. Letty kicked the shotgun toward the washing machine and walked to the edge of the wine cellar, breathing through her mouth; she could taste the rotten air, now tinged with cordite.

She looked at Arnold. "I'm going to call an ambulance for you."

He nodded frantically at the pistol in Letty's hand.

"You want me to . . . ?"

He let out a long, low moan—sad and desperate and inhuman.

"Arnie," she said, raising the Beretta, "I'm not sure even you deserve this."

10

Letty walked down the long driveway toward the 4Runner. The rain had stopped and the clouds were breaking up, a few meager stars shining in the southern sky, a night bird singing to a piece of the moon. For a fleeting moment, she felt the heart-tug of having witnessed a beautiful thing, but a crushing thought replaced the joy—there was so much beauty in the world, and in her thirty-six years, she'd brushed up against so little of it.

At the bottom of the driveway, she took her phone out of the ruined handbag, but, five seconds into the search for Chase Rochefort's number, powered off her phone. She'd done enough. So very much more than enough.

The alarm squeaked and the 4Runner's headlights shot two brief cylinders of light through what mist still lingered in the cul-de-sac. Letty climbed in behind the wheel and fired up the engine. Sped away from that house, from lives that were no longer her problem. Felt a familiar swelling in her chest, that core of inner strength she always seemed to locate on the first night of a long bit when the loneliness in the cell was a living thing.

And she promised herself that she'd never try to be good again.

Only harder, stronger, truer, and at peace, once and forever at peace, with her beautiful, lawless self.

A NOTE FROM BLAKE CROUCH ON "THE PAIN OF OTHERS"

"The Pain of Others" is the Letty Dobesh story that most closely follows the television show. The pilot episode of *Good Behavior* is based largely on what you just read, with the exception of a few key changes.

First: Arnold in the short story becomes Javier in the TV show.

The short story and the pilot episode run pretty close to parallel until the beginning of chapter 8. In both the show and the story, Letty leaves Daphne's house with Daphne armed, angry, and in total control of her would-be assassin.

In the story, Arnold suffers an unimaginably awful fate. He's essentially tortured for days in Daphne's basement. The twist in the story is that Daphne turns out to be a monster and Letty comes to a stark realization: maybe she shouldn't have interfered with Chase and Arnold's deal.

But in thinking about the show, Chad Hodge and I realized that this ending wouldn't work. First, it leaned too heavily into horror territory, which wasn't the tone we wanted to strike. But more critically, what intrigued us most about the Letty-Arnold (soon to be Letty-Javier) dynamic was the intensity of their connection. When we meet Letty, she's just out of prison, struggling with addiction, stealing, self-hating, basically on the brink of a massive implosion. The idea that this fucked-up relationship with a contract killer might actually save her from herself felt like a big idea to us. It felt like the kind of show we wanted to make. "*Bonnie and Clyde* from Bonnie's perspective" is how we pitched it to networks.

Of course, there were other additions to the pilot episode, since we wanted to establish all of Letty's world and the people who populated it, right out of the gate. So we meet her mother, Estelle, a character who

vices: theft

3/12/09

What if mark kills everyone?
manipulate protag too. Could be 8K

* * *

Possible Scenes

① Thief hiding in room after trying to rob it,
overhears hitman & client from closet or
shower.

② Thief at diner. Meets hitman (patron). Flirts.
Decides to go home with him to get info
on mark.

③ Thief & hitman at hotel room. Hook-up.
Her thoughts. Tension... trying, finally succeeding
to get info on the mark.

④ Thief goes to mark with information. To
warn her. At her house perhaps. Do they hide
from hitman? Incredibly tense. Mark (& baby?)
escape? (very subtle clues... photos of kids
passed)

Blake Crouch's handwritten notes from 2009, listing ideas for scenes that have remained remarkably consistent across the novella The Pain of Others *and the pilot episode of* Good Behavior, *titled* "So You're Not an English Teacher."

is original to the show. Letty's son, Jacob. And finally, her parole officer, Christian.

I'm often asked how Chad and I approach the process of cowriting a script. We figured out an egalitarian method (well, to be fair, it was Chad's idea).

A television script is approximately fifty to sixty pages. Chad would write the first ten pages. I would then read and edit what he'd written, write the next ten pages, and send it back to him. Then we'd rinse, wash, repeat, sending pages back and forth in this manner until the first episode was finished. It took us about a month to write the first draft.

The hotel where most of the short story takes place is an actual hotel in Asheville, North Carolina, called the Grove Park Inn. I have never stayed the night there, but I've been in its lobby and always admired the architecture, which, as Cormac McCarthy describes it in his genius novel *Suttree*, looks like an "old rough pile of rocks."

We tried to shoot our exterior and interior lobby locations at the Grove Park Inn, but alas, we were filming in North Carolina at the peak of fall foliage, and the hotel was booked too solidly for us to film there.

We shot in Wilmington instead, down on the North Carolina coast, which served us just fine.

The opening shot of the TV series shows rain pouring down in front of a diner at night and the words "Statesville, North Carolina" superimposed on the screen. Statesville is a town in the Piedmont of North Carolina, where I was born.

The director of the pilot episode is a brilliant Danish woman named Charlotte Sieling. A few months out from the first day of principal photography, when we were still trying to figure out the visual look of the show, Charlotte called and said, "I think I know what we are going to do. We are going to create something called 'poetic noir.'"

"Great," we said. "What the hell is 'poetic noir'?"

And she said, "I have no idea. I'll tell you when we're finished."

SUNSET
KEY

Letty Dobesh came in from the cold to the smell of cooking eggs, bacon, and stale coffee. The Waffle House was in a bad neighborhood in south Atlanta near the airport. She wore a thrift-store trench coat that still smelled of mothballs. Her stomach rumbled. She scanned the restaurant, dizzy with hunger. Her head throbbed. She didn't want to meet with Javier. The man scared her. He scared a lot of people. But she had $12.23 in her checking account and she hadn't eaten in two days. The allure of a free meal was too much to pass up.

She had come twenty minutes early, but he was already there. He sat in a corner booth with a view of the street and the entrance. Watching her. She forced a smile and walked unsteadily down the aisle beside the counter. The points of her heels clicked on the nicotine-stained linoleum.

Sliding into the booth across from Javier, she nodded hello. He had short black hair and flawless brown skin. Every time they'd met, Letty thought of that saying, *Eyes are windows to the soul.* Because Javier's weren't. They didn't reveal anything—so clear and blue they seemed fake. Like a pair of rhinestones, with nothing human behind them.

An ancient waitress sidled up to their table with a notepad and a bad perm.

"Get y'all something?"

Letty looked at Javier and raised an eyebrow.

He said, "On me."

"The farmer's breakfast. Extra side of sausages. Egg whites. Can you make a red eye? And a side of yogurt."

The waitress turned to Javier.

"And for you, sweetie?"

"Sweetie?"

"What would you like to order, sir?"

"I'll just eat her fumes. And a water."

"Ice?" The way she said it sounded like "ass."

"Surprise me."

When the waitress had left, Javier studied Letty.

He said finally, "Your cheekbones look like they could cut glass. I thought you'd come into some money."

"I did."

"And what? You smoked it all?"

Letty looked at the table.

She held her hands in her lap so he wouldn't see the tremors.

"Let me see your teeth," he said.

"What?"

"Your teeth. Show me."

She showed him.

"I'm clean now," she whispered.

"For how long?"

"A month."

"Don't lie to me."

"Four days."

"Because you ran out of money?"

She looked toward the open grill. She was so hungry she could barely stand it.

"Where are you staying?" Javier asked.

"Motel a few blocks away. It's only paid for through tomorrow."

"Then what? The streets?"

"You said you had something for me."

"You're in no condition."

"For what, a beauty pageant? I will be."

"I don't think so."

"Jav." She reached across the table and grabbed his hand. He looked down at it and then up at her. Letty let go like she'd touched a burning stovetop. "I need this," she whispered.

"I don't."

The waitress returned with Javier's water and Letty's coffee, said, "Food'll be right up."

"It's only day four," Letty said. "Another week, I'll be as good as new. When's the job?"

"It's too big to risk on a strung-out *puta*."

Anyone else, Letty would have fired back with some acid of her own. Instead, she just repeated her question: "When is it?"

"Eight days."

"I'll be fine. Better than."

He watched her through those unreadable eyes.

Said finally, "Would you risk your life for a million-dollar payday? I'm not talking about getting caught. Or going to prison. I mean the real chance of being killed."

Letty didn't even hesitate. "Yes. Javier, have I ever let you down?"

"Would you be sitting here breathing if you had?"

Javier looked out the window. Across the street stood a row of storefronts. A pawnshop. A hair salon. A liquor store. Bars down all the windows. There was no one out under the gray winter sky. The roads had already been salted in advance of a rare southern ice storm.

"I like you, Letty. I'm not sure why."

"You're not going to ask me why I do this to myself—"

"I don't care." He looked back at her. She could see he'd made a decision. "Letty, if you fail me—"

"Trust me, I know."

"May I finish?" He reached into his water and plucked out a cube of ice. Pushed it around on the table as it slowly melted. "I won't even bother with you. I'll go to Jacob first. And when you see me again, I'll have a part of him to show you."

She drew in a sudden breath. "How do you know about him?"

"Does it matter?"

The last two months of this crystal bender, she hadn't allowed herself to think about her son. He'd been taken from her just prior to her last incarceration. He lived in Oregon with his father's mother. Six years old. She pushed the thought of him into that heavy steel cage inside her chest where she carried more than a little hurt.

The food came. She wiped her eyes.

She tried not to eat too fast but she had never been hungrier in her life. It was the first time she'd had real food in her stomach in days. Waves of nausea swept over her. Javier reached across the table and stole a strip of bacon.

"Bacon tax." He smiled and bit it in half. "Have you heard of a man named John Fitch?"

She didn't look up from the scrambled eggs she was shoveling into her mouth. "No."

"He was the CEO of PowerTech."

"What's that?"

"A global energy-and-commodities company based in Houston."

"Wait, maybe I did see something about it on the news. There was a scandal, right?"

"They cooked the books, defrauded investors. Thousands of PowerTech employees lost their pensions. Fitch and his inner circle were behind it all. A month ago, he was convicted for securities fraud. Sentenced to twenty-six years in prison."

"What he deserves."

"Says the thief. He's out on a seventy-five-million-dollar bail. Scheduled to report to a federal prison in North Carolina in nine days."

Letty set her fork down and took a sip of black coffee. She hadn't had caffeine in weeks, and already she was feeling jittery. "Where's this going, Jav?"

"Fitch's family has abandoned him. He has no one. He's sixty-six and will very likely die in prison. I happen to know that he's looking for some female companionship for his last night of freedom. Not a call girl from some"—Letty was already shaking her head—"high-end escort service. Someone very, very special."

"I'm not a prostitute," Letty said. "I've never done that, never will. I don't care how much money you wave in my face."

"Do you think I couldn't find a woman who is younger, more beautiful, and more . . . *experienced* . . . than you if all I wanted was a hooker?"

"Charming."

"Letty, this could be the score of a lifetime for you."

"I'm not following."

Javier smiled, a terrifying spectacle.

The entire restaurant shook as a jet thundered overhead.

"It's not a trick," he said. "It's a heist."

The last work Letty had done with Javier had involved stealing from high rollers in Vegas. He'd hooked her up with universal keycards and supplied surveillance to let her know when a mark had left their room. That job had presented a degree of risk for sure, but nothing beyond her comfort level. Nothing like this.

She cut into a waffle and said, "Gotta be honest—I'm not over the moon about the word 'heist.'"

"No? It's one of my favorites."

"It sounds like something you need a gun for. And a getaway car. The type of job where people get killed."

She swabbed the piece of waffle through a pool of syrup and took a bite.

"See, that's the beautiful thing about this job, Letty. It's high return on a low-risk venture."

"You just asked me if I'd be willing to *risk my life* for a million-dollar payday."

"I didn't say there was no risk. Just that it's low considering the potential payout."

"Do you have any idea how many times I've heard that, and then the opposite proved to be—"

"Are you accusing me of glossing over risk in our prior dealings?"

Letty realized with a jolt of panic that she'd insulted him. Not a wise course. Javier didn't get angry. He just killed people. The stories she'd heard were the stuff of legend.

"I guess not." She backtracked. "It's just that I've been burned in the past. But not by you. You've always been on the level with me."

"I'm glad you see that. So would you like to hear me out, or should I leave?"

"Please continue."

"Fitch is spending his last days on his private island fifteen miles south of Key West. Most of his property has been lost to forfeiture to pay back the victims. However, I have a man in Fitch's security detail. He tells me there's something of great value at Fitch's residence in the Keys."

The waitress stopped at the booth and freshened up Letty's coffee. When she was gone, Letty stared across the table at Javier.

"Well, do I have to guess?" she asked.

He glanced around the restaurant as he reached into his leather jacket. The sheet of paper he pulled out had been folded. Javier slid it across the table. Letty pushed her plate aside and opened it.

She stared down at a painting printed in full color from a Wikipedia page—a skull with a burning cigarette in its mouth.

"What's this?" Letty asked.

"*Skull with Burning Cigarette.* You familiar with your postimpressionists?"

"Not so much."

"You don't recognize the style?"

"I'm a thief, not an art collector."

"But you have heard of Vincent van Gogh . . ."

"Of course."

"He painted this one in the mid-1880s."

"Good for him."

"The original is hanging in Fitch's office in the Keys."

"Get to the good part."

Letty managed to smile through her driving headache.

"When we discuss the value," Javier said, "we're talking about two numbers. First, what could we sell it for at auction? In 1990, Van Gogh's *Portrait of Dr. Gachet* sold for eighty million. In adjusted dollars, that's a hundred and forty."

Letty felt something catch inside her chest. It was a strange sensation, like being dealt four aces. She fought to maintain her poker face.

"You said there were *two* numbers?" she asked.

"Obviously, we can't just steal this painting and put it up for a public auction through Sotheby's."

"Black market?"

"I already have a buyer."

"How much?"

"Fifteen million."

"What did Fitch pay for it?"

"Doesn't matter. We're selling it for fifteen. You're rolling your eyes over fifteen mil? Really?"

"I just think we can—"

"You have no idea what you're talking about. Look at me." She looked at him. "You don't know me well. But from what you do know, do you honestly believe I would broker a deal for anything less than the most favorable payout to me? To my crew?"

When she didn't respond right away, he continued, "The answer you're looking for is 'no.' That should leave you with one question."

"What's my cut?"

"Two."

It was more money than Letty had ever imagined acquiring in a lifetime of theft, but she forced herself to shake her head. Strictly on principle of not accepting a first offer, if nothing else.

"No?" Javier seemed amused. "Two isn't a fair cut for a tweaker?"

"That's not even fifteen percent of the take, Jav."

"You think it's just you and me on this deal? That there aren't some other people I have to pay off? You wouldn't even have this opportunity without me. Sounds like you'd be living in a box somewhere."

"Why do you need me? Why not have your guy on the inside handle this?"

"That was the initial plan, but he was let go last week."

"Why?"

"Nothing related to this."

"So you *had* a man on the inside."

"This can still work, Letty. I can get you on that island with all the tools, all the intel you'll need."

She sighed.

"What?" he asked. "What are you thinking?"

"I'm thinking you might have put this together, but I'll be taking on most of the risk."

Javier cocked his head as if he might disagree.

Instead, he held up four fingers and then waved her off before she could respond. "I know it's hard for you, but just accept graciously, Letty. It'll buy you enough crystal to kill yourself a thousand times over."

"Go to hell."

Javier reached into his jacket again and tossed a blank white envelope on the table.

Letty opened the flap, peered inside.

A bunch of fifties and an airline ticket.

"You fly down to Miami a week from today," Javier said. "I'll be there to pick you up. There's a thousand in there. I assume that'll cover you until then?"

"Yeah."

She didn't even see his arm move. Suddenly, Javier had a grip on the envelope. She instinctively pulled back, but he wouldn't let go.

"Just so we're clear," he said, "this is for your room and board. And to get yourself a world-class makeover. Keep receipts for every purchase.

If you use this money to buy meth . . . If you look anything like the car crash that's sitting across the table from me when you get off the plane in Miami . . . You know how this will end."

3

Letty walked back to her motel through the falling sleet. It made a dry, steady hiss drumming against the sidewalk. It was bitter cold. The streets were empty.

The thousand in her pocket kept whispering to her. *Take a detour down Parker Street. Score a teener. You'll still have time to get straight before Florida. You've got to celebrate. This could be the best thing that's ever happened to you. To Jacob.*

As she crossed Parker, she glanced down the street. Caught a glimpse of Big Tim standing on his corner, unmistakable in a giant down parka, designer jeans, fresh kicks.

She ached to score, but instead focused her gaze back on the road ahead.

Kept walking.

By the time she unlocked the door to her dingy motel room, Letty was freezing. She punched on the television and headed toward the bathroom. The local news was in hysterical-storm-coverage mode.

She drew a hot bath. The tub filled slowly, steam peeling off the surface of the water. Letty stripped out of her clothes. She stood naked in front of the mirror that hung from a nail on the back of the door. A crack ran down through the glass. It somehow seemed fitting.

She'd never looked so thin. So haggard. In health, she was a beautiful woman with clear eyes the color of amber. Short auburn hair. Curves in all the right places.

Now, the shape of her skeleton was emerging.

For a split second, Letty had the strong sense of her old self, her real self, her best self, trapped inside the emaciated monster staring back at her.

It took her breath away.

One week later, Javier picked Letty up in a black Escalade curbside at Miami International. They headed south into the Keys on the Overseas Highway, which crossed the 110-mile island chain. The stereo system blasted Bach's four lute suites on classical guitar. Letty leaned her head against the tinted glass and watched the world go by.

Land and sea. Land and sea.

On the far side of Key Largo, Javier glanced across the center console.

He said, "You don't even look like the same woman."

"Amazing what a little mud rinse can do."

"Your eyes are clear. Your color's good."

"I put on ten pounds since you saw me last. Got my hair and nails done. I did a whole spa thing yesterday. I wasn't sure what to wear for tomorrow . . ."

"I brought your dress. I brought everything you'll need."

Letty couldn't remember the last time she'd seen the ocean. More than ten years ago at least. The sea was blue green and the sky straight blue and scattered with clouds that resembled puffs of popped corn. It was early afternoon. Short-sleeve weather. "Winter" felt like a word that had no meaning here.

They rode through Islamorada and Layton.

Quaint island villages.

Past Marathon, they crossed Seven Mile Bridge into the Lower Keys.

The views into the Gulf of Mexico and the Straits of Florida went on forever.

They reached Key West in the late afternoon and Javier checked Letty into the La Concha Hotel. She tried to lie down and rest but her mind wouldn't stop. She poured herself a merlot from the minibar and went to the table by the window. The breeze coming through the screen smelled like cigar smoke and sour beer. And the sea.

She sat drinking and watching the evening come.

Her room on the fifth floor overlooked Duval Street. The street was crowded with cars and bicycles. Tourists jammed the sidewalks. She heard a ukulele playing in the distance. On many rooftops, people had gathered to watch the sunset. She wondered what it would feel like to be here on vacation. To have no plans beyond finding a place for dinner. To be in paradise with someone you loved.

She didn't have to see Javier until lunch tomorrow, when they would make their final preparations. So Letty slipped into a new skirt and tank top and headed out into the evening.

There was an atmosphere of celebration.

Everyone happy and loaded. Nobody alone.

At the first intersection, she left the chaos of Duval Street. Two blocks brought her into a residential quarter. It was an old neighborhood. She passed restored bungalows and Caribbean-style mansions.

On every block, there was at least one house party going.

Ten minutes from the hotel, she found a Cuban restaurant tucked away in a cul-de-sac.

The hostess told her it would be a ninety-minute wait.

There was a patio out back with a tiki bar, and Letty installed herself on the last available stool.

The noise was considerable.

She didn't like being here alone.

She opened her phone and tapped out texts to no one.

It took five minutes for the barkeep to come around. He was an old salt—tall and thin. So grizzled he looked like he'd been here back when Ponce de León first showed up. Letty ordered a vodka martini. While he shook it, she eavesdropped on a conversation between an older couple seated beside her. They sounded midwestern. The man was talking about someone named John, and how much he wished John had been with them today. They had gone snorkeling in the Dry Tortugas. The woman chastised her husband for getting roasted in the sun, but he expertly steered the conversation away from himself. They talked about other places they'd been together. Their top three bottles of wine. Their top three sunsets. How much they were looking forward to a return trip to Italy. How much they were looking forward to Christmas next week with their children and grandchildren. These people had seen the world. They had loved and laughed and lived.

Letty felt a white-hot hate welling up in the pit of her stomach.

She didn't even bother to persuade herself it wasn't jealousy.

The barkeep set her martini down. A big, sturdy glass the size of a bowl. The drink had been beautifully made with flakes of ice across the surface.

"Wanna start a tab?"

"No."

"Twelve dollars."

Letty dug a twenty out of her purse.

The barkeep went for change.

The gentleman beside her had worn a sports coat for the evening. In the light of the surrounding torches, Letty could see by the cut it was designer. Gucci or Hugo Boss. She could also see the bulge of a wallet in the side pocket. So easy to lift. Two moves. Tip over her martini glass in the man's direction and slip her hand into his blazer pocket as he reached for a napkin to help clean up. She'd done it a dozen times and only once did the mark ignore the spill.

And that'll really make you feel better? To drop a bomb on their holiday?

When she stole, it was out of necessity. Only ever about the money. She'd never made it personal. Survival had been her sole motivation, even at her lowest points. Never the intentional infliction of hurt to boost her own morale.

While the old barkeep was still at the register, Letty slipped off the chair, leaving her drink untouched.

She threaded her way between tables, out of the restaurant, and onto the street.

By the time she reached Duval, she had managed to stop crying.

Her life seemed to be defined by moments like these.

Moments of pure self-hatred.

And this was just one more in a long, long line.

"You slept okay?" Javier asked.

"Yes."

"How are you feeling?"

"All right. Nervous."

"Good."

"Good?"

"Nerves keep you sharp."

Wind rustled the fronds of the palm tree that overhung their table. They were sitting outside at a café two blocks from the ocean. A cruise liner had just unloaded gobs of people onto the island. They were streaming past on the sidewalk. Herds of Hawaiian shirts and Panama hats propelled by pasty-white legs.

"You should eat something," Javier said.

Their waiter had brought their lunches five minutes ago, but Letty hadn't touched her ham-and-brie panini or her salad.

"I'm not hungry."

"Eat."

She started picking at her salad.

Between bites, she pointed the tines of her fork at the surface of the table, where Javier had placed a cardboard box.

"Is that my dress?"

"Among other things."

"Is it pretty?" she asked in a mock-girlish voice.

He ignored this. "In the box, you'll find a mini spray bottle. The label says 'breath freshener.' It's an opiate tincture. Oxycodone. Fitch is a wine snob. Five squirts in his wineglass during dinner. Not four. Not six. Exactly five."

"Got it."

"Get him to his room before he starts to fade. His people will hang back if they think you've gone in there to sleep with him."

"How thoughtful."

"Once he's unconscious, head up to the office. Now listen to me very carefully. My contact says there will be five men on the island. Three outside. Two in the residence. Considering his notoriety, Fitch has had countless death threats and one actual attempt. These men are private security contractors. Ex-Blackwater types. They've all seen combat. They'll be armed. You won't be."

"Where will you be during all this?"

"I'm getting there. Part of your outfit is a Movado watch."

"Ooohhh, Christmas."

"Don't get attached. It's on loan. We rendezvous at eight on the eastern tip of the island. You won't be allowed to bring your cell phone. Keep an eye on your watch." He patted the box. "There's also a map of the island and blueprints of the house. I would've given them to you earlier, but I just got my hands on them."

"What if I get held up?"

"Don't get held up."

"Eight. All right. How are we getting off the island?"

"A Donzi 22 Classic Shelby. I'm picking it up after we're done here."

"Is that a boat or a plane?"

"It's a boat."

"Fast?"

"Faster than any of Fitch's watercraft. *Miami Vice* fast."

"Assuming this works, what'll stop them from just radioing for help? Having the coast guard track us down on the way back to Key West?"

"You are taking on some risk here, which is why I will tolerate these questions that seem to suggest I haven't thought everything through. That I haven't foreseen every possible glitch and planned accordingly." Javier took a sip from his glass of ice water. "We won't be going back to Key West. We'll be heading five miles farther south to a deserted key in international waters."

Letty forced herself to take a bite of the sandwich.

Javier said, "Now we haven't even discussed the most important part of this. The reason we're all here."

"Skull with Burning Cigarette."

"The painting is hanging in Fitch's office on the wall behind his desk. My intel is that there's no theft-security system. You just have to cut it out of the frame."

"Cut it?"

"Careful. Like shooting-heroin-into-your-femoral-artery careful. There's a razor blade hidden in the bottom of your handbag under a piece of black electrical tape."

"I'm not comfortable with that," Letty said.

"Why?"

"Because they'll probably search the handbag, don't you think?"

"Where do you want to hide it?"

"I'll think of something. What kind of bag is it?"

"Try to control yourself. Louis Vuitton."

"Up to this point, the accessories are far and away the best part of this job. That, I keep."

"We'll see."

"And once I get the canvas out of the frame?"

"Roll it up. You'll find a plastic tube taped to the underside of Fitch's desk. Stick the rolled-up canvas inside and get yourself to the eastern edge of the island."

"What about cameras?"

"None."

"What about the people who actually see me up close? Who can identify me and describe me to law enforcement?"

"You'll be a redhead tonight."

"That's it?"

"What do you want, a latex mask? This isn't *Mission: Impossible*. This is the price you pay for a shot at four million dollars."

Letty felt something go cold at the base of her spine.

Without exception, this was the most dangerous job she'd ever signed on for.

Javier said, "You wondering why I don't just slip in there while you're distracting Fitch?"

"Now that you mention it."

"Because that would turn this into a very different kind of job. People would die. I assume you don't want that."

"No."

Javier tossed his napkin onto the table. He stood and looked at his watch.

"It's almost two thirty. They're picking you up outside the hotel at four." He pulled out his money clip and dropped two twenties on the table. "Go back to your hotel. Study your maps. Get your head right for this."

Letty had barely touched her food.

Javier stared down at her through a pair of aviator sunglasses.

"You forgot something," she said.

"What's that?"

"My name. Who will they be expecting?"

"Selena Kitt. S-E-L-E-N-A K-I-T-T. But you won't be carrying any identification."

"And my backstory? Should he be so inquisitive?"

"Thought I'd leave that to you. Bullshit seems to flow so freely from your lips. Moments like this don't come along very often," he said.

"I know."

"Ship sails at four. Make me proud, Letisha."

6

Riding down to the lobby, Letty watched herself in the reflection of the elevator doors. So did the twenty-year-old boy with an obvious hangover standing beside her. She didn't blame him. She looked stunning. The little black dress was Chanel. The fuck-me pumps were Jimmy Choo. They made her legs look like stilts. She'd worn wigs before but nothing as finely made as this one—wavy red hair that fell just past her shoulders. Javier certainly had a well-developed sense of style, but she couldn't imagine he'd put this ensemble together all by himself.

The elevator doors spread apart. Letty tried to steady her breathing as she walked out into the lobby, past a grouping of palm trees in planters.

She glanced at her watch.

3:58.

As she approached the revolving door at the entrance, a man stood up from a leather chair. He wore a black suit and carried the beefy build of a bouncer. Bald, graying goatee, and a sharp skepticism in his eyes. She figured the extra padding under his jacket for a shoulder holster.

"Ms. Kitt?"

"The one and only."

The man extended his hand and she shook it. "I'm James. I'll be taking you to Mr. Fitch. Right this way."

He led her outside to a silver Yukon Denali idling on the curb and opened a rear passenger door. Letty climbed in. The driver didn't bother to introduce himself. He wore sunglasses and a black suit almost identical to James's. He was younger, with a buzz cut and the strong, chiseled jaw that Letty associated with soldiers.

The radio was tuned to NPR and turned down so low that Letty could barely hear it.

James sat beside her.

As they pulled out into traffic, he reached behind them into the cargo area and emerged with a black leather writing pad. He opened it and handed Letty a sheet of legal-size paper. At the bottom, she noticed a line for the signature of Selena Kitt.

"What's this?" she asked.

"A nondisclosure agreement."

"For what?"

"For anything that happens from the moment you climbed into this vehicle until you're returned to Key West."

She studied the document.

"Looks like a bunch of legalese."

"Pretty much."

"You wanna give me the CliffsNotes since I didn't go to law school?"

"It says that you agree not to disclose any details regarding your time with Mr. Fitch. Not in writing. Not in conversation with anyone. And if you do, you can be sued for breach of contract in accordance with the laws of the state of Florida."

"You mean I can't write a tell-all book and then sell the movie rights about Mr. Fitch's last night of freedom?" She smiled to convey the intended humor, but James just tapped the signature line with a meaty finger.

"Sign right here, please."

They parked at a marina on the west coast of the island, not far from the hotel. Letty walked between her escorts to the end of a long dock. Waited for several minutes while the men took in the mooring lines on a fifty-foot yacht. When they'd prepped the boat for departure, the driver climbed to the bridge. James offered Letty a hand and pulled her aboard. He led her up several steps and through a glass door into a salon.

The pure luxury stopped her in her tracks and took her breath away.

"Please make yourself comfortable," James said, gesturing to a wraparound sofa.

Letty eased down onto the cool white vinyl.

"Would you care for a drink?" he asked.

She knew she shouldn't, but she felt so jittery she figured just one wouldn't hurt. Might even help to calm her down.

Letty peered around James at a wet bar stocked with strictly high-end booze.

"I see you've got Chopin," she said.

"Rocks?"

"Yes."

"With a twist?"

"No, thank you."

James crossed the teak floor to the freezer and took out a bucket of ice. Letty leaned back into the cushion and crossed her legs. The engines grumbled to life deep inside the hull. At the bar, James scooped ice cubes into a rocks glass and poured. He brought her drink over with a napkin.

"Thank you, James."

He unbuttoned his black jacket and sat down beside her.

She could feel the subtle rocking as the yacht taxied out into the marina.

There were windows everywhere, natural light streaming in through the glass. The view was of a colony of sailboat masts, the dwindling shoreline of Key West, and the sea.

Letty sipped her drink. The vodka was nearly flavorless in her mouth with a slight peppery burn going down.

"That's very good." She set her glass on the coffee table.

"We need to have a conversation," James said.

"Okay."

"You're aware of who your client is?"

"Mr. Estrada explained everything to me."

"This is a very important night for Mr. Fitch."

"I understand that."

"And you're here for one reason, Ms. Kitt. To make it as special and as memorable as it can possibly be." Letty was nodding, waiting for a pause to break eye contact. But James's stare held hers. She couldn't help feeling they were the eyes of a cop. Hopefully an ex-cop. "There are a few topics of conversation that are off-limits," he continued. "You are not to bring up the case against Mr. Fitch, his trial, or his conviction in any way. You are not to discuss his sentence or anything relating to the prison term he's facing."

"Okay."

"You will not discuss anything you've read in the papers or on the Internet. You will not discuss your view of his guilt or innocence."

"I have no views. No opinions whatsoever."

"Now I need you to stand up for a minute."

"Why?"

"Just do it, please."

Letty uncrossed her legs and stood.

James got up as well and faced her.

"Hold your arms out."

"Are you frisking me?"

"That's exactly what I'm doing. Mr. Fitch has received numerous death threats since the case against him was filed."

"And you think I'm packing something in this itty bitty dress?"

"Hold your arms out horizontal to the floor."

Letty did as she was told and stared out the window while James patted her down, his hands roving over every nook and cranny.

"Jesus, at least buy me dinner first."

"All right, you can sit, but I will need to search your purse."

Letty handed over the Louis Vuitton.

The yacht exited the marina. The engines roared to life as they throttled out into open water. She could feel the tension in her gut ratcheting up a notch. Having never learned to swim, being surrounded by water always made her uneasy.

She tried not to watch too intently as James opened the handbag. He removed the contents, one at a time, and lined them up on the coffee table.

Lipstick.

Mascara.

Package of Kleenex.

Hotel keycard.

He paused as he lifted out the mini spray bottle.

"What's this?" he asked.

Letty's heart stomped in her chest.

"Just what it says. Breath freshener."

James held it up to the light, read the label. "Watermelon?"

"Try it if you like."

James let slip a tight smile and set the bottle on the table. Then he dumped out the remaining items: a condom, a mirror, brush, gum, and two hair bands.

"You left your cell phone. Good."

James held the interior of the handbag up to the window so the sunlight could strike the black textile lining.

After a moment of close inspection, he handed her the bag, said, "I apologize for the intrusion. We should be arriving in less than twenty minutes."

James walked out of the salon. She heard him talking quietly into his cell phone.

Letty returned everything to her purse and settled back into the cushion with her glass. She sipped her drink and turned her thoughts to this man she would be spending the coming hours with. From everything she'd read, Fitch was a monster. His conspiracy and fraud had resulted in the bankruptcy of PowerTech. Fifteen thousand employees lost their jobs. Many lost their life savings. Investors in PowerTech lost billions.

Throughout his prosecution, Fitch had always maintained that he just wanted the chance to tell his story. But at crunch time on the witness stand, he'd invoked the Fifth Amendment to avoid self-incrimination.

The yacht hummed along at over forty knots, skimming the water like a blade across ice.

Key West was nothing but a blurred line of green on the horizon.

Out here, there was nothing but the sea in all its varying hues of blue and jade. Its surface sparkled. The horizon lay sprinkled with tiny islands. The sky shone a deep, cloudless blue. It was early evening. They cruised straight into a red and watery sun.

Letty could feel the vodka buzz coming on like a soft warmth behind her eyes. A numbness in her legs. For a fleeting second, everything seemed so impossibly surreal.

This yacht.

This thing she was about to do.

This life she lived.

The sea in the vicinity of Fitch's island was shallow. His dock extended seventy-five yards out from the shore into water just deep enough to berth a boat.

Letty followed James out of the salon onto the stern.

A tall, thin man stood on the last plank of the dock. He was throwing squid into the sea, his gray hair blowing in the breeze. He wore a white long-sleeved shirt unbuttoned to his sternum. White Dockers. Leather sandals. Very tan. He finished rinsing off his hands under a faucet mounted to the end of the wharf and dried them with a towel as Letty approached. Reaching down, he gave her a hand up onto the dock. He was even taller than she'd first thought. Six-two. Maybe six-three. He smelled of an exotic cologne—sandalwood, spice, jasmine, lime, money.

The man still hadn't let go of her hand. His fingers were cool and moist, as soft as silk.

"Welcome to Sunset Key, Selena. Please call me Johnny."

She could hear Texas in his voice, but it wasn't overbearing. Houston drawl by way of an Ivy League education. She stared up into his face. Smooth-shaven. No glasses. Perfect teeth. He didn't look sixty-six years old.

"It's beautiful here, Johnny," she said.

"I like to think so. But it pales in comparison to you. They broke the mold."

Letty riveted her eyes on what he'd been feeding and saw gray fins slicing through the water.

"Sand sharks," Fitch said. "Not to worry. Totally harmless. They like the reefs for protection. A mother and her pups."

He offered his arm. They walked down the long dock. Letty could see the cupola of a house peeking above the scrub oak that covered the island. According to the blueprints and to Javier, that was Fitch's office.

"How was your ride over?" Johnny asked.

"Wonderful. Your yacht is amazing."

"Part of my midlife crisis, some would say."

Letty glanced back over her shoulder.

James and the unnamed driver followed at a respectful distance.

"Don't give them another thought," Fitch said. "I know James searched you, and I apologize for that barbarous invasion, but it couldn't be helped."

"It was no big deal," she said.

"Well, you're *my* guest now."

"I'm glad to hear it," Letty said. "You've lived here long?"

"Back in my former life, I was primarily based in Houston. I also had a winter place in Aspen. An apartment in Manhattan. Of course, those are gone now. But I bought this key about twenty years ago when it was fourteen acres of unspoiled paradise. Designed the house myself. It was always my favorite. There's a view of the sea from every room."

They went ashore.

A man of fifty or so stood waiting for them in khaki slacks and a short-sleeved button-down.

"Selena, this is Manuel, my caretaker and steward. He's been with me for . . . how long, Manuel?"

"Since you buy island. I live here twenty-two years."

Fitch said, "Before we go to the house, I thought we'd take a walk on the beach." He kicked off his sandals.

Manuel turned to Letty. "If you give me shoes, I take them up to house for you."

Letty leaned over and unfastened her pumps. She stepped out and handed them to Manuel.

"And your purse?"

"I think I'll hang on to this."

Fitch said, "Thank you, Manuel."

"Very good, sir."

"You're leaving for Key West when Angie goes?"

"Yes, I go with her."

"Take care, my old friend."

Letty and Fitch walked barefoot up a man-made beach.

"Manuel came over on a raft. Half of them died. Sends his paychecks back to Havana. He's an honorable man. Loyal. He'll never have to work again after tomorrow. He doesn't know this yet."

The sand was soft and stark white and still warm from the sun. There was no surf, no waves. No boats within earshot. You could hear the sound of leaves rustling, a bird singing in the interior of the island, and little else. The water was bright green.

Fitch picked up a shell before Letty stepped on it.

He said, "'Down on the seashore I found a shell, left by the tide in its noonday swell. Only a white shell out of the sea, yet it bore sweet memories up to me. Of a shore where brighter shells are strown, where I stood in the breakers, but not alone.'"

"That's lovely," Letty said.

They moved on up the shore. It seemed that with every passing second, the sun expanded, its pool of light coloring a distant reef of clouds.

"This is why I chose the Keys, you know," Fitch said. "Best sunsets in the world. Ah. Here we are." They had reached the tip of the island. A pair of Adirondack chairs waited in the sand under the shade of a coconut palm. They faced west, an ice bucket and a small wooden box between them.

Letty and Fitch crossed the sand to the chairs. The sunset spread across the horizon like a range of orange mountains. There was no wind. The water as still as glass.

Letty glanced down at the box. The top had been stamped:

Heidsieck & C° Monopole
Goût Américain
Vintage 1907
N° 1931

Fitch pulled an unlabeled bottle out of the ice water. He held it to the fading light. The glass was green and scuffed. He went to work opening it.

Letty said, "Special. Even has its own box."

"This bottle was on its way to the Russian royal family when the boat carrying it was torpedoed by Germans. What must have gone through those young sailors' minds? It took a half hour: they knew, for a half hour, they were going to die and could do nothing to stop it. Nothing but wait and watch the minutes slide."

"In what year?"

"In 1916. The vintage is 1907, which makes this—"

"A hundred and nine years old?" He nodded. "Oh my God."

"It was recovered from the wreck eighteen years ago. The bottles were perfectly preserved at the bottom of the ocean. Notable not only for the rarity and the history, but, as it turns out, the wine itself is quite excellent. I bought one for a special occasion. I'd say tonight qualifies. Would you get the glasses, please?"

Letty reached into the box and lifted out two crystal flutes.

"Go ahead and ask," Fitch said as he struggled with the cork.

"Ask what?"

He worked it out so slowly, there was no pop. Just a short hiss as the pressure released. The cork crumbled in his hand. He held the opening of the bottle to her nose.

It smelled like perfume.

"What do you think?" he asked.

"Gorgeous."

Fitch took a whiff himself and then began to pour.

"So ask," he said. "It won't offend me."

"What?"

"What I paid."

"That would be rude."

"But you want to know."

With her glass full, Letty smelled it again, the carbonation bubbles misting her nose.

"All right. What'd you pay, Johnny?"

"Two hundred and seventy-five thousand dollars. Here's to you," he said.

She didn't even know how to comprehend such a figure.

"To you, Johnny."

They clinked glasses.

The champagne was amazing.

"I want to know your passion, Selena."

"My passion?"

"What is it that most excites you in this life? What is your prime mover? Your reason for being here?"

"Prada."

This got a huge laugh.

"Money can't buy you happiness, darling. Believe me, I've tried."

"But it affords your own brand of misery."

"You're a lively one, Selena. Let's sit back and enjoy, shall we?" Fitch said. "This is going to be a night for the senses."

Letty leaned back in her chair. "That's the prettiest sunset I've ever seen," she said.

"I'm just glad it didn't rain."

Fitch laughed but there was a sadness in it.

All the color went out of the sky.

"Where are you from, Selena?" Fitch asked.

Letty had only had two glasses, but she felt good. Too good. "A little bit of everywhere. I guess I don't really think of any one place as home."

Fitch looked over at her. He patted her hand.

"I know this must be a strange deal for you," he said.

"It's not."

"You're kind to say that, but . . ." He stared out across the sea. With the sun gone, there were only shades of blue. "I'm just really glad you're here tonight."

◆

They walked toward the house on a sandy path that cut through the heart of the island.

Letty held Fitch's hand.

"You have a real sweetness about you, Selena," he said. "Reminds me of my wife."

"You miss her? No, I'm sorry. That's not my business."

"It's all right. I brought her up. Yeah, I miss her. She left me a year and a half ago."

"Before your trial."

"Go through something like this, you find out real quick who your friends are. It's not always your kin. Only real loyalty I've seen is from Manuel and my lawyers. Both of whom I pay. So what does that tell you? Two of my sons won't speak to me. My youngest only communicates by e-mail. I understand to a point, I guess. I've put them through a lot. Do you have children, Selena?"

"I have a son," Letty said before it even crossed her mind to lie.

"Is he in your life?"

"He's not."

Through the underbrush, Letty caught a glimpse of houselights in the distance.

Fitch said, "But is there anything he could do that would make you stop loving him?"

"No."

"Anything that would make you willingly abandon him?"

"Absolutely not."

"I suppose our kids don't love us quite like we love them."

"I hope that's not true."

"I've had my fair share of company over to the island. You're different, Selena."

"I hope you mean that in a good way."

Fitch stopped. He turned and faced her and pulled her body into his.

"I mean it in the best way."

It took her by surprise when he leaned down for a kiss.

Not the kiss itself, but the pang of guilt that ripped through her like a razor-tipped arrow.

The house was a large gray box set on foundation piers. It had long eaves and wraparound decks on the first and second levels. Extensive latticework enclosed the space under the stairs. Letty spotted rafts and plastic sand-castle molds. Snorkeling gear. Life jackets. Beach toys that she imagined hadn't been touched in years.

She and Fitch rinsed the sand off their feet at the bottom of the stairs. Halfway up, Letty could already smell supper cooking.

As they walked through the door, Fitch called out, "Smells wonderful, Angie!"

Letty followed him into an open living space. Hardwood floors. Exposed timber beams high above. The walls covered in art deco. A giant marlin had been mounted over the fireplace. A live-jazz album whispered in the background. There were candles everywhere. The bulbs in the track lighting shone down softer than starlight.

"You have a lovely home, Johnny."

Letty spotted James and another man walking down a corridor. She and Fitch passed a spiral staircase. They arrived at a granite bar that ran the length of the gourmet kitchen. A stocky woman in a chef coat slid something into a double oven. She wiped her brow off on her sleeve and came over.

"Selena, meet Angie," Fitch said.

"Hello," Letty said.

"Angie is head chef at a Michelin-starred restaurant in Paris. I flew her over to prepare something special for tonight. How's it coming, Angie?"

"I can bring out starters whenever you're ready."

Fitch glanced at Letty. "Hungry?"

"Starving."

"We're ready," he said.

"How about wine?"

"Yes, I think we'd like to have some wine. You decanted everything I showed you?"

"They're in the cellar, ready to go. What would you like to start with?"

"Bring out the 1990 Pétrus, the '82 Château Lafite Rothschild, and the '47 Latour à Pomerol."

"Quite a lineup," Angie said.

"So much good wine to drink, so little time. We'd like to taste everything side by side, so bring six glasses."

"You aren't trying to get me drunk, are you?" Letty teased, bumping her shoulder into Fitch's arm.

"Now why would I need to do that?"

They sat at an intimate table in a corner, surrounded by windows.

In the candlelight, Fitch looked even younger.

Letty dropped her handbag on the floor between her chair and the wall.

Angie brought the wine in three trips, carrying the empty bottle in one hand and a crystal decanter in the other.

All of the bordeaux was astonishing. With wine like this in the world, Letty didn't know how she could ever go back to seven-dollar bottles of merlot from the supermarket.

They started with a plate of plain white truffles.

Then foie gras.

Then scallops.

Angie kept bringing more courses. Because Letty was drinking out of three glasses, she had difficulty gauging her intake. She tried to pace herself with small sips, but it was all simply the best thing she'd ever tasted.

Over the cheese course, Fitch said, "It occurs to me there will be many evenings to come when I long to return to this meal."

Letty reached across the table and took hold of his hand.

"Let's try to stay in the moment, huh?"

"Sound advice."

"So, Johnny. What is your passion?"

"My passion?"

"For a man who has achieved all the material wants."

"Experience." His eyes began to tear. "I want to experience everything."

Angie came over to the table. "How was everything?"

"I'm speechless," Fitch said.

He rose out of his seat and embraced the chef. Letty heard him whisper, "I can't thank you enough for this. You're an artist, and the memory of this meal will sustain me for years to come."

"It was my pleasure, Johnny. Dessert will be up in fifteen."

"We're done here, and we can handle getting dessert for ourselves. Someone will clean up. You've been cooking all day. Why don't you take off."

"No, let me finish out the service."

"Angie." Fitch took hold of her arm. "I insist. Pete's waiting in the yacht to take you back."

For a moment, Letty thought she might resist. Instead, the chef embraced Fitch again, said, "You take care of yourself, Johnny."

Fitch watched her cross to the front door.

As she opened it, she called out, "Dessert dishes and silverware are on the counter beside the oven! Good night, Johnny!"

"Night, Angie!"

The door slammed after her, and for a moment, the house stood absolutely silent.

Fitch sat down.

He said, "How strange to know you've just seen a friend for the last time."

He sipped his wine.

Letty looked out the window.

The moon was rising out of the sea. In its light, she could see the profile of a suited man walking down a path toward the shore.

"It begins to go so fast," Fitch said.

"What?"

"Time. You cling to every second. Savor everything. Wish you'd lived all your days like this. Excuse me."

He rose from his seat. Letty watched him shuffle across to the other side of the room and disappear through a door, which he closed after him.

She lifted her purse into her lap and tore it open. Her fingers moved with sufficient clumsiness to convince her she'd gotten herself drunk. She grasped the spray bottle. Fitch still had some wine left in two of his glasses. Reaching across the table, she put five squirts into the one on the left.

The door Fitch had gone through creaked open.

He emerged cradling a bottle in one arm and carrying two glasses in the other.

He was grinning.

From across the room, he held up the bottle, said, "The jewel of our evening. Come on over here, sugar."

Fitch sat down on a leather sofa.

Letty still hadn't moved, her mind scrambling.

I missed my chance. I missed my chance.

9

Fitch waved her over. "Sit with me!"

Letty glanced at her watch as she stood.

7:05.

Fifty-five minutes until her rendezvous with Javier at the east end of the island.

She grabbed one of her wineglasses and Fitch's.

He was already tugging the cork out of the bottle as she walked over.

Letty said, "Here you go and leave, and I was just on the verge of making a beautiful toast." She tried to hand Fitch his wineglass.

"We'll toast with this instead," he said, showing her the bottle—Macallan 1926.

"Oh, I'm not too much of a scotch girl."

"I understand, but this is really something. You couldn't *not* love this."

"Now I'm losing my nerve."

She thought she registered a flash of something behind his eyes—rage? But they quickly softened. Fitch put the bottle down and accepted his glass and stood.

Letty had no idea of what to say.

She looked up at Fitch and smiled, her mind blank.

It came to her in an instant—a toast she'd overheard at a wedding she'd crashed two years ago. Back then, she'd spent her Saturdays stealing presents from brides and grooms. She'd developed something akin to an X-ray sense for determining the most expensive gifts based solely on wrapping paper.

She raised her glass.

"Johnny."

"Selena."

"'May a pack of blessings light upon thy back.'"

"Ah, Shakespeare. Lovely."

Letty watched as he polished off the last two ounces of his wine. They sat on the sofa. Fitch opened the scotch and poured them each two fingers into heavy tumblers.

He put his arm around Letty. She cuddled in close. He went on for a minute about the rarity of this spirit they were about to imbibe. He was drunk, beginning to ramble. She finally sipped the scotch. It was good. Better than any whiskey she'd ever tasted, but she hadn't lied. She just wasn't a scotch girl.

After a while, he said, "Everything I've ever done, I've done for my family, Selena. Everything."

Sitting with Fitch on the sofa, it hit her again. That old, familiar enemy. Regret. Guilt. Her conscience. Truth was, she liked Fitch. If for no other reason than he was facing a lifetime behind bars with grace. Making the most of his final hours of freedom. She tried to remind herself of all the people Fitch had hurt. And it wasn't like he'd be hanging this painting she was about to steal on the walls of his prison cell.

But the arguments rang hollow. Insincere.

After a while, she felt his head dip toward hers.

He was saying something about his family, about how everything had always been for them. His eyes were wet. He didn't sound drunk so much as sleepy.

Letty set her glass on the coffee table and eased Fitch's out of his grasp.

"What're you doing?" he slurred.

Letty stood and took him by the hand. She pulled him up off the couch.

"Come with me," she whispered.

"My drink." His eyes were heavy.

"You can always finish your drink." She pressed up against him and wrapped her arms around his neck. "Don't you want *me*, Johnny?" She kissed him with passion this time—openmouthed and long. Hoped it would give him enough of a charge to make it into bed.

She led him through the living room.

"Where's your room?" she whispered even though she knew from the blueprints that it was very likely the large master suite on this level. He pointed toward the opening to a hallway just behind the spiral staircase.

They stumbled down a wide corridor. The walls were covered with photos of Fitch's family. One in particular caught Letty's eye as she passed by. It had been taken out on the deck of this house, fifteen, maybe twenty years ago—a much-younger Fitch standing with three teenage boys. All shirtless and tanned. Mrs. Fitch in a bathing suit. The sea empty, huge, and glittering behind them.

Letty dragged Fitch through the doorway of his bedroom and shut the door behind them. The suite was sprawling. There was a flat-screen television mounted to the wall across from the bed. A bookcase. A small desk where she spotted a laptop, a cell phone, and an empty wineglass. Floor-to-ceiling windows looked out over the dock. French doors opened onto the deck. She couldn't see the moon from here, but she could see its light falling on the sea.

"Go lie down," she said.

Fitch staggered toward the bed.

Letty took her time pulling the curtains.

Fitch mumbled, "You're so . . . beautiful."

"That's what my daddy used to tell me." She could feel the push of adrenaline cutting through her intoxication. "I just need to step into your bathroom for a moment," she said. "I'll be right out. You get comfortable."

He said, "We don't have to do anything. Unless you want to." The words came too soft, too muddled.

Letty walked into the bathroom. She shut the door, hit the light.

It was bigger than most apartments she'd lived in. Leaning over the sink, she studied her pupils in the mirror. They were black and huge. She sat down on the toilet and took a deep breath. All the things she needed to do in the next forty-five minutes pressed down on her. She took herself through all the steps. Pictured it happening perfectly.

Five minutes passed.

She went to the door.

Pulled it open as softly as she could manage and slipped back into Fitch's room.

The wood-paneled walls now glowed with a soft warmth from candles on the bedside tables. They smelled like vanilla. The hardwood creaked as she crossed to the foot of Fitch's bed.

The old man lay on his back with his arms and legs spread out. His shirt was unbuttoned, his pants pulled down to his knees. It was as far as he'd gotten. He snored quietly, his chest rising and falling.

He looked tragic.

"Bye, Johnny," Letty whispered.

Then she moaned several times.

Full-voiced and throaty.

Hoping that would keep Fitch's men away from his room for the time being.

10

The bedroom door opened smoothly, without a sound. She moved in bare feet down the corridor. All of the doors she passed were cracked. The rooms dark. Where the hallway opened into the main living area, she stopped. The spiral staircase was straight ahead, but hushed voices crept around a blind corner. It sounded like they were coming from the kitchen. For a moment, she stood listening. Two men. They were eating, probably picking through the leftovers.

Letty went quietly up the staircase, taking the steps two at a time.

Near the top, she caught a view down into the kitchen. It was James and some other black-suited man with long hair who she hadn't seen before. They stood at the counter, dipping crackers into the foie gras.

She came to the second floor. A long hallway, empty and dark, branched off from either side of the spiral staircase. The blueprints indicated that this level housed four bedrooms, two bathrooms, and a study. Letty kept climbing, using the iron railing as a guide. The noise of the men in the kitchen fell farther and farther away. By the time she reached the final step, she couldn't even hear them.

Letty stepped into the cupola of the house.

Because three of the walls consisted entirely of windows, the moon poured inside like a floodlight.

Letty ripped off the wig. She ran her hands carefully through her hair until her fingers found the razor blade.

Padding over to the desk, she turned on a lamp.

Her watch read 7:35.

She stared up at the wall above the desk.

What the hell?

She'd been expecting to see the Van Gogh—a skeleton smoking a cigarette. What hung on the wall instead was an acrylic of a horse. Maudlin colors. Proportions all wrong. She was no art critic, but she felt certain this painting was very badly done.

Leaning in close, she read the artist's signature in the bottom right-hand corner of the canvas.

Margaret Fitch

Letty sat down in the leather chair behind the desk. Her head dizzy and untethered. Had Javier told her the wrong place to look? Had she somehow misunderstood him? No, this was Fitch's office. In fact, there should be a plastic tube taped beneath the desktop. She reached under, groping in the darkness. All she felt was the underside of the middle drawer.

Assumptions.

Somewhere, she'd made a false one.

The blueprints had identified the cupola as an office, but maybe Fitch's was actually down on the second floor.

That had to be it.

She spun the swivel chair around and started to rise.

Took in a hard, fast breath instead.

A shadow stood at the top of the spiral staircase, watching her.

11

For a long minute, Letty couldn't move.

Her heart banged in her chest like a mental patient in a rubber room.

"Dear old Mom did that one," Fitch said. "God rest her soul." He pointed to the painting of the horse behind his desk. "She gave it to me for Christmas fifteen years ago. I hated it at the time, and with good reason. Let's be honest. It's hideous. So I kept it in a closet, except for when she visited. Then I'd have to swap out my Van Gogh for that monstrosity. Make sure she noticed it proudly displayed in my office."

"Johnny . . ."

"And then she died, and I got sentimental. I sold *Skull with Burning Cigarette* and put *My Horse, Bella* on that wall permanently. It's been there for five years, and every time I look at it, I think of my mother. I've even come to appreciate certain aspects of it."

Fitch took a step forward into the splay of light emanating from the desk lamp. He looked clear-eyed. He held a large-caliber revolver in his right hand. His glass of Macallan in the other. "There are similarities between you and Van Gogh, Letisha. Both fiery redheads, with a nasty predilection for self-injury. Suffering from what the psychoanalysts would best describe as 'daddy issues.' And, perhaps most pityingly, both masters of a trade you would never be appreciated for. At least, not in life.

"You look confused, Letty." Fitch smiled. "Yes, I know your real name. I like it more than your alias, if you want to know the truth. Although I did prefer you as a redhead."

He sipped his scotch.

"Did you call the police?" she asked.

He laughed. "I'm going to see my fair share of law enforcement for the rest of my life, don't you think? The notion that you'd try to steal from me? Come onto my island and steal from me, you brazen girl."

"Johnny." Letty thought she might be just drunk enough to scare up some real emotion. She had disarmed plenty of men in the past with a few tears.

"Oh, don't cry, Letty."

"I'm sorry, Johnny. I tried to take advantage of you, and—"

"No, no, no. I should be the one apologizing to you."

She didn't like the sound of that. Something in the tone of his voice suggesting a piece of knowledge she wasn't privy to.

"What are you talking about?" she asked, starting to get up.

"No, you just stay right there, please."

She settled back into the chair.

"My life," Fitch said, "has been so rich. So . . . fragrant. I went to Yale undergrad. Harvard business. I was a Rhodes scholar. Earned a PhD in economics from Stanford. I lived in Europe. The Middle East. Argentina. I rose as fast through the ranks of PowerTech as anyone in the history of the company."

Fitch edged closer, his hair trembling in the breeze stirred up by a pair of ceiling fans.

"By thirty-five, I was the youngest CEO of any global energy company in the world. I had a family I loved. Mistresses on six continents. I was responsible for twenty-four thousand employees. I brokered multi-billion-dollar deals. Destroyed both domestic and foreign competitors.

I've fucked in the Lincoln bedroom under three separate presidencies. I've been adored. Demonized. Admired. Copied. I've played hard. Made men and ruined men. Had the finest of everything. More money than God. More sex than Sinatra. Trust me when I say I go to federal prison for the rest of my life a happy man. If the masses knew how much pure fun it is to have this kind of power and wealth, they'd kill me or themselves."

He walked to one of the windows and stared out across the moonlit sea.

"You're a beautiful woman, Letty Dobesh. In another life . . . who knows? But I didn't allow you to come into my home for sex. I've had plenty of that." He held up his tumbler. "And I don't really even care about this forty-thousand-dollar bottle of single malt. On the last night of a man's life . . . before he reports to prison for a twenty-six-year stint that will likely kill him . . . he has to ask himself: What do I do with these last precious moments? Do I revisit the things in life that most made me happy? Or use this last gasp of freedom to have a truly new experience?"

Letty eyed the staircase.

If she hadn't been drunk, she could've probably reached the steps before Fitch turned and fired. But he was holding a beast of a gun. A .44 Magnum or worse. Taking a bullet from something of that caliber would finish her.

"What does this have to do with me?" she asked.

Fitch turned and faced her.

"Sugar, there's one thing I've never done. I was too old for the draft in 1969. I've never been to war, which means I've never had the experience of taking a life."

"He'll kill you," she said. "Even in prison, he can get to you."

"Are you talking about Mr. Estrada?"

She nodded.

"You don't see it yet, do you?"

"See what?"

"It was Javier who put this whole thing together, Letty. There was never any painting. No drug in your breath freshener spray. I told him about this last experience I wanted to have before I went away, and for a very significant price, he brought you to me."

Letty felt a surge of hot bile lurch out of her stomach—anger and fear.

She fought it back down.

"Johnny . . ."

"What? You going to beg me not to do this? Try to test the limits of my conscience? Good luck with that."

"It won't be how you think. It's not some great rush."

"See, you don't understand me. I have no expectations of feeling one way or another. I just want to have done it. What's a richly lived life that has never caused death? You ever killed someone, Letty?"

"Yes."

"How was it?"

"Self-defense."

"Kill or be killed?"

She nodded.

"Well, how was it?"

"I think about it every day."

"Exactly. Because you had a true experience. And that's all I want. This is how it'll work. I'm going to wait right here for five minutes. Give you a head start. See, I don't just want to kill you, Letty. I want to hunt you."

"You're as evil as they say."

"This is not about good and evil. I've lived dangerously all of my life. I want to continue to do so on this final night, when it counts the most. My security team is on their way down the dock as we speak. They're going to anchor my speedboat a quarter mile out. My yacht is staying in the marina in Key West for the night. It'll just be you and me on the island. I know you can't swim, Letty. That was one of the requirements that, unfortunately for you, landed you this job. So there are no ways off this little island."

"I have a son," she said.

"Haven't we covered that already?"

"Johnny, please." Letty stood up slowly and moved forward with her arms outstretched, hands open. "Has it occurred to you you aren't thinking clearly? That you have all this emotion swarming around inside of you and—"

Fitch pointed the revolver at her face and thumbed back the hammer.

"That's close enough." It wasn't the first or the second or even the third time she'd had a firearm pointed at her. But she never got used to that gaping black hole. Couldn't take her eyes off of it. If Fitch chose to pull the trigger in this moment, it was the last thing she'd ever see.

"You destroyed thousands of lives," she said, "but you aren't a murderer, Johnny."

"You're right. Not yet. Now you have four minutes."

12

Letty raced down the spiral staircase.

Drunk.

Terrified.

Still trying to wrap her head around what had just happened.

Only one conclusion: Javier had played her.

Sold her out.

She passed the second floor and ran down the remaining steps into the living room. Straight to the cordless phone on a bookshelf constructed from pieces of driftwood. She grabbed the handset off its base, punched "Talk."

Fitch was already on the other end of the line: "I'm afraid that's not going to work, Letty. Three minutes, thirty seconds. Twenty-nine. Twenty-eight . . ."

I need a weapon.

She dropped the phone and turned the corner into the kitchen, started yanking drawers open.

As she pulled open the third, she saw it lying on a butcher-block cutting board next to a pile of onion and garlic skin. A chef's knife with a stainless handle and an eight-inch blade.

For ten seconds, she stood in the remnants of Angie's cooking, trying to process her next move. So much fear coursing through her she felt paralyzed.

There were dishes everywhere.

A tart cooling on the granite beside the oven.

Water dripping from the faucet.

Fitch expected her to run. Expected to chase her across the island. So should she stay in the house? Hide in a bedroom on the second floor and let him wander around outside in vain?

Decide. You can't just keep standing here.

Grabbing the knife, she bolted across the room into the foyer. Jerked open the front door. Slammed it shut after her. She shot down the steps, wondering which way to go. The shore seemed like a bad idea. She headed into the interior of the island, staying off the path, fighting through undergrowth. Gnarled branches clawed at her arms. Ripped tears in her Chanel dress. Her bare feet crunched leaves and tracked through patches of dirt. She'd barely made it fifty yards when a blinding pain seared the sole of her right foot.

Letty went down with the knife, clutching her foot.

In the moonlight that filtered through the leaves, she studied the damage. The underside of her foot had been starred with a dozen sandspurs. She began pulling them out one at a time. Wincing. Wondering how many minutes she had left. Less than two? Less than one?

The sound of the front door creaking open on its salt-rusted hinges answered her question.

She looked up.

All she could see was the top half of Fitch standing on the deck. When he reached back to shut the door, she noticed that he wore a strange-looking hat. He lowered out of view, the steps groaning as he descended.

Letty dug the last few spurs out of her foot.

She could hear Fitch approaching.

Footsteps and heavy breathing.

She didn't move.

Figured Fitch had to be walking up the path. It didn't sound like he was thrashing through undergrowth.

Letty inched back farther under the shadow of the scrub oak. Tucked her chin into her knees and tried to make herself as small as possible.

Fitch passed within twenty feet.

She crouched there, listening, until his footfalls could no longer be heard.

Letty crawled out from under the oak and came to her feet.

Total silence.

The stars shining.

The moon still climbing in the sky.

She knew what the shore on the dockside of the island was like from that sunset stroll. A narrow strip of beach lined with vegetation. No place to hide.

She moved slowly through the scrub oak, taking care that her shoulders didn't brush against the branches. She crested the midpoint. The island sloped gently down to the opposite shore. This side struck her as more wild. There was no beach. Just mangroves all the way down to the water.

She squeezed her way through the slim trunks. The mangroves grew more densely clustered as she neared the shore. Letty crawled on hands and knees now. The foliage above her head so thick it blotted out the sky, only splotches of moonlight scattered across the ground.

She went on until the trees were too close to go any farther.

They boxed her in like prison bars.

Lying on the ground, her body twisted between the mangroves, she finally breathed deep and slow.

The temperature hovered in the upper sixties, but she shivered, covered in sweat. Her dress had been shredded climbing through the mangroves. It hung from her shoulders in tatters.

She felt good about this spot. Considering it was night, she was all but invisible. And Fitch would have a hell of a time reaching her. She couldn't imagine the old man, who had at least ten inches on her, fitting through this grove of tightly packed trees. How big had he said this island was? Fourteen acres? Best-case scenario, she could hole up here for the night. Fitch had to report to prison tomorrow. If she could survive until then . . .

Letty glanced at her watch. The tips of the hour and minute hands glowed in the dark.

8:15.

She should've met Javier at the east end of the island with fifteen million dollars in a plastic tube. This should've been the most exhilarating, life-changing score of her life. Instead she was being hunted down like a dog. Because she'd put her faith in a psychopath. Because, again, her judgment had failed.

Something niggled her.

A seemingly small fact she was overlooking.

A rodent scurried through some leaves nearby.

A mosquito whined in her ear.

What was it?

No flashlight.

That was it.

Fitch hadn't brought a flashlight outside with him. When she'd glimpsed him walking down the steps, she'd expected to see a light wink on. But it never did. And then he'd just strolled up that path in the dark like—

Her breath caught in her chest.

—like he could see.

She sat up.

That wasn't a strange-looking hat he'd been wearing. Those were night-vision goggles.

Thirty, forty yards away—impossible to know for sure—Letty heard branches rustling.

It was the sound of something big coming her way through the underbrush.

Get out of here now.

Letty started pushing her way through the labyrinth of mangroves. By the time she broke free onto higher ground, her little black dress dangled by a thread.

An oak branch beside her face snapped off.

The gunshot followed a microsecond later.

A boom like a clap of thunder.

And she was running.

Arms pumping.

Gasping.

Driven by pure instinct.

She ducked to miss an overhanging branch, but another one caught her across the forehead.

Blood poured down into her face.

She didn't stop.

There were lights in the distance.

The house.

She veered toward it. At least inside, Fitch wouldn't have the sight advantage he held right now.

Letty came out of the scrub oak and onto the dirt path that cut down the middle of the island. For three seconds, she paused. Hadn't had this much physical exertion in months. Her lungs screamed. She could hear Fitch closing in.

Letty opened up into a full sprint as she approached the house.

She reached the stairs, grabbed the railing.

Three steps up, she stopped. Maybe it was a premonition. Maybe it was just a feeling. Something whispered in her ear, *You go in that house, you won't ever come out alive.*

She backed down the steps and stared into the darkness under the stairs. Thinking, *Where is the last place in the world he would expect someone to hide who can't swim?*

Her eyes fell upon the snorkel set hanging from a nail driven into the concrete.

She grabbed the snorkel and mask and took off running toward the east end of the island—the only side of it she hadn't seen.

She shot back into the scrub oak. Glancing over her shoulder, she spotted Fitch coming into the illumination of the floodlights mounted to the deck. He pulled off the goggles to pass through the light. Held them in one hand, that giant revolver in the other. A big, sloppy grin spreading across his face like a kid playing cowboys and Indians.

Another fifty yards through the oak, and then Letty was standing on the shore in her strapless bra and panties. Her Chanel had been ripped off completely.

The water looked oil black.

She could hear Fitch coming.

She wondered how much time she had.

Wanting to do anything but wade out into the sea.

13

Letty dropped the knife on the shore, pulled on the mask, and stepped into the water. It was cool, just south of seventy-five degrees, and shallow. She took invisible steps, no idea if the next would plunge her in over her head or shred her feet on coral.

By the time she'd gone thirty feet out from the shore, the water came to her knees. At fifty feet, it reached her waist. She stopped, couldn't force herself to take another step. Hated the feel of it all around her, enclosing her. Reminded her in so many ways of death.

Fitch stumbled out of the oak onto the beach. He stood profiled in the moonlight. He was looking all around as Letty jammed the snorkel into her mouth and slowly lowered herself into the sea. Struggling not to make a splash or a ripple.

The water rose above her chest.

Then her neck.

Up the sides of her face.

Daddy, please.

She could breathe, but still she felt as though she were drowning. No sound underwater but her own hyperventilation as she sucked oxygen down the tube at a frantic pace.

Her knees touched the sandy bottom of the ocean floor.

The claustrophobia was unbearable.

Even with her eyes wide open, she couldn't see a thing.

Lifting her right arm, she fingered the top of the snorkel. It stuck two inches out of the water. She pushed with her knees, rose up slowly until the top half of the mask peeked above the surface.

Fitch still stood on the shore, staring in her direction.

She dipped back under.

It was unbearable.

Nine years old.

The cool and the dark of it.

By herself at night in the single-wide trailer she shares with her father. He comes home from the bars. Drunk and angry and alone. He loves to take hot baths when he's drunk, but Letty has beaten him to it. He finds her soaking. With their water heater on its last leg, it will take two hours to heat enough for another bath. In a rage, he shatters the fluorescent bulb over the sink and locks her inside. Tells her through the door if she gets out of that bath before he says she can, he'll drown her in it.

It's wintertime. Four hours later the water is cold and the air temperature in the bathroom even colder. Letty sits with her knees drawn into her chest, shivering uncontrollably. She's crying, calling for her father to let her out. Pleading with him for forgiveness.

Toward dawn, he kicks the door in. From the smell of him, he's somehow drunker than before.

She says, "Daddy, please."

It happens so fast. She doesn't even see him move. One minute she's shivering and staring up at him. The next he's holding her head under the frigid bathwater, telling her what a bad girl she is to make him so angry. He's beaten her before. He's come after her with a broken beer bottle. With his belt. With his fists. With other things. But she has never believed she was going to die.

Because there was no warning, she didn't have a chance to take in a full breath of air. Already bright spots are blooming behind her eyes, and she's struggling, kicking. Wasting precious oxygen. But his boot heel press down hard against her back. Pinning her to the fiberglass. He holds her head down with two hands. Even drunk, he has the strength of an ox. The build of a diesel mechanic. She is no match. Every second passing so slowly. Panic setting in. Thinking, He's going to kill me. He's really going to kill me this time.

The fear and the horror meet in a single, desperate need. Breathe. Breathe. Breathe. *She can't help it. Can't resist the pure, burning desire. She takes a desperate breath just as her father jerks her head out of the water by her hair.* "Think you learned a lesson?" *he growls.*

She nods, apologizing as she bawls hysterically out of the only emotion her father has ever caused in her—fear.

There are other nights like this. A handful of them are worse. She will never learn to swim. Will always fear the cold, dark water. Will never understand despite a thousand sleepless nights why her own father hated her.

And like that nine-year-old girl, a part of her still believed it was her fault. Some flaw in her emotional chemistry. And nothing she could do, no amount of logic, no quantity of love from anyone, would ever make her stop believing it.

Letty came up suddenly out of the ocean.

If Fitch saw her and shot her, so be it. But she couldn't stand another second underwater.

He was gone.

She spit out the snorkel's mouthpiece. Took several careful steps toward the shore until the water level had dropped to her thighs. She stared down the north and south beaches—too dark to see much of anything.

Backing away, she settled down into the water until only her head was above the surface.

Waited.

Five minutes slipped by.

Twenty.

It was beyond quiet.

She watched the moon on its arcing path over the island.

So thirsty, her head pounding from the booze.

After a long time, she heard footsteps crunching in the sand.

Letty backed into deeper water and lowered herself once more until only her eyes were exposed.

Fitch trudged up the north beach and arrived at the end of the island. He stopped and waited, listening.

Letty forced herself back under.

When she came up a minute later, Fitch had started down the south side of the island.

Fitch has to report to prison tomorrow. If I can survive until then . . .

She returned to that comforting thought she'd had in the mangroves. The idea that if she survived until tomorrow, until Fitch was gone, she would be in the clear.

Is this another assumption that's going to get me killed?

Fitch's security detail had played a part in this. Exactly how much they knew was uncertain, but they were culpable. Fitch's life would be over tomorrow, but theirs would carry on. If the old man didn't close the deal, could she really expect this force of ex–military contractors to leave this loose thread dangling?

Another impulse of fear swept through her.

A new realization setting in.

Hiding all night from Fitch might not be enough to save her life.

14

Letty stood up and walked out of the sea, the taste of salt water on her tongue. When she reached the shore, she pulled off the mask and dropped it and the snorkel in the sand. She picked up the knife. Headed quickly down the south beach. The fear fell away, anger rushing in to fill the void.

She could see Fitch in the distance—his white shirt bright as day in the moonlight. He walked sixty yards ahead and she was gaining on him, keeping close to the trees that lined the beach in case Fitch suddenly spun around. Her footfalls in the soft white sand were soundless. She picked up her pace, moving now at a full run. The wind blowing her skin dry. The faster she ran, the angrier she got, the less afraid she felt.

Fitch was almost to the dock, Letty only twenty yards back from him now. Her legs ached from the full-on sprint. Her lungs burned. Tears streamed out of the corners of her eyes.

She knew exactly what had triggered it.

Being down under that cool December water.

How could she not think of Daddy? Dead twenty years and yet still with her. Always with her. She'd heard somewhere that every person reaches a certain age and, though they keep getting older, they never feel any older.

In so many ways, she was still that nine-year-old girl shivering in cold bathwater.

In prison, she'd sat through enough AA and NA meetings to know the drill.

The propaganda.

Admit a lack of control.

Acknowledge a higher power.

Make amends.

Embrace forgiveness.

That was all fine and good. But at the end of the day, the nine-year-old trapped in this woman's body couldn't care less about twelve steps. Her world was imbalanced in the worst possible way—she'd had a monster for a father. If she lived to be a hundred, she would never get past it.

Up ahead, Fitch stepped across the dock.

Letty slowed from a sprint to a jog, trying to mask her accelerated breathing.

She leapt over the sand-blasted planks.

Took the final steps slow and careful.

Fitch held the revolver in his right hand. His gait looked tired, like an old man's.

Letty tightened her grip on the knife and pushed the point of the blade into his back.

Fitch took a sudden breath and quit walking.

She said, "I'll shove it through to your stomach. Drop the gun, I swear to God."

He still held the gun. Letty leaned her weight into the blade, and as it started to penetrate, the revolver hit the sand.

She lunged down for the gun and let go of the knife as she swiped it up.

Stumbled back away from Fitch.

The revolver was a giant thing. Must have weighed four or five pounds. It was nickel-plated and over a foot long with "Raging Bull" engraved down the side of the barrel.

Letty had to struggle to keep it leveled on Fitch's chest.

"You just stay right there," Letty said, backing another foot away.

Four cartridges remained in the cylinder.

"You lost your lovely dress," Fitch said.

"Get down on your knees."

Fitch carefully lowered himself into the sand. "That's a big gun for a little girl. Packs a helluva kick."

It took two fingers to pull the hammer back.

"Wasn't personal," Fitch said, the pitch of his voice kicking up a few degrees. "I hope you understand that. You are formidable, little girl. A scrapper. In another life, I'd have you come work for me."

"Why is that all I ever hear anytime somebody does me wrong? Nothing's ever personal anymore. All those people you ripped off . . . that wasn't personal either, was it? Just business, right?"

"Letty—"

"No, you've explained yourself plenty. Your men are offshore in boats?"

"Yes."

"Are there any other boats on the island?"

"No."

"Do you have your cell phone with you?"

"No."

"We're going to the house."

"Why?"

"Get up. Start walking."

"Calling the police would be a very bad idea, Letty."

"Get. Up."

Slowly, Fitch stood.

"Now walk over to the dock," she said. "And do it slowly with your hands raised."

But Fitch didn't move. He just stared at her.

"Do you think I'll tell you again?" she asked.

"I knew. I knew it all along. From the minute I met you—this would be one hell of a night, Letisha. Rare to feel I've met my match."

He let slip a long, tired breath.

Like he'd come to the end of something.

And sprang at Letty.

It was the loudest gunshot she had ever heard, with a kick like a shotgun.

Fitch sat in the sand, his mouth dropped open. He made a sucking sound, as if trying to draw breath. The hole in the dead center of his chest was massive. Letty was shaking. Fitch fell back onto the beach and stared up at the stars. There was so much blood she knew he was going to die.

Out on the water, a motor growled to life.

Letty turned around. She looked down the dock and out to sea.

A single spotlight glided toward her, the motor getting louder as it approached. Soon, she could see the profile of the speedboat. It was seconds away from reaching the end of the dock.

Letty sprinted inland. Already, she could hear men's voices behind her. Shouting her name. Her real name. Ordering her to stop as their shoes pounded against the planks.

She tore up the steps onto the deck and shouldered through the front door.

After several hours in the dark, the onslaught of light made her eyes water.

Letty barged into the living area and rushed to the cordless phone. It was still lying on the floor where she'd dropped it. She grabbed it, hit "Talk," held it to her ear.

Beep-beep-beep-beep-beep-beep-beep-beep—

She raced down the hallway into Fitch's bedroom.

Slammed the door after her, locked it, flipped the lights.

Thank God.

There it was.

Lying on the desk.

She picked up Fitch's cell phone, praying it still held a charge.

Outside, she could hear numerous sets of footsteps hammering up the stairs.

Men screaming her name.

They charged into the house.

Hide.

Letty crossed the hardwood floor to the French doors.

Someone was coming down the hall.

She turned the handle.

Locked.

The knob on the other door rattled—someone trying to get in.

She was out of time.

Nothing left to do but fight.

Three bullets versus three or four men.

She thought, *This may be how it ends for you. Are you ready?*

The door splintered, a man kicking it in from the other side.

She aimed the revolver at the bedroom door.

After two more kicks, it burst open, and the muscled girth of James filled the doorway. His cheeks were flushed from running. With one arm, Letty trained the Raging Bull on his substantial center mass. In her other hand, she gripped the cell phone.

Her thumb keyed in 911.

James held a black pistol at his side. At least for the moment, he was smart enough to keep it there.

Someone on the second floor yelled his name.

"Down here!" he shouted back.

"You got her?"

"Sort of!"

Letty moved her thumb toward the "Call" button.

As the other men came running, James said, "Who you calling?"

"Nine-one-one."

"Why don't we talk about that, okay?"

Letty's right biceps had begun to cramp from holding the Raging Bull with one arm.

She could hear the other men in the hallway now.

James yelled over his shoulder, "Everybody stay back!"

"What exactly do we have to talk about?" she asked.

"How dialing that number is going to get you killed."

"Way I figure, I'm dead either way."

"That's not true. But if you involve the Monroe County Sheriff's Office, we're going to have a problem. Why don't you put that gun down. I'll do the same. And we'll talk."

"I'm not putting anything down. You people tried to kill me."

"What if I were to guarantee your safety?"

"I'd call bullshit."

"You put the gun down. I'll get you some clothes. And I'll have you back on Key West within the hour."

"You must think I'm really stupid."

"No, ma'am." He shook his head. "This can work out for everyone. Of course, you'd have to do a few things for me."

"Like?"

"Like never mention any of this to anybody. Ever."

"What about that famous dead man on the beach? Aren't some people expecting him tomorrow?"

"We can damage-control the mess you made of Mr. Fitch."

"The mess *I* made."

"It's you I'm worried about."

Over James's shoulder, Letty spotted a man creeping into view.

"Your buddy right behind you is about to get you shot, James."

"Go sit in the living room!" he yelled. "All of you!"

"James—"

"Right now, Scott."

She heard them falling back.

James looked at her. "Better?"

"For some reason, I don't think you'd be so interested in talking to me if I didn't have this big goddamn hand cannon pointed at your chest."

"Now that's just not true. You put it down and see."

"I don't think so. Tell me again how you're planning to *damage-control* your boss."

"If all goes well," James said. "If you and me don't have a big shoot-out . . . you'll see some breaking news tomorrow morning. Go something like this . . . Convicted CEO of PowerTech found dead on his private beach. He took his own life the night before he was scheduled to report to prison. There will even be a suicide note."

"Oh, you can fake his handwriting, too?"

"No, he already wrote it."

Letty didn't want to, but her strength was failing. She set the cell phone on the floor at her feet and took a two-handed grip on the revolver.

"Asking yourself why he might've done such a thing?" James asked. "Regardless of what you may think of him, Fitch is a brilliant man. He saw this as a possible outcome of what he had planned for tonight. He didn't want anyone to take the fall. Not me or the other guys. And not even you, the woman who killed him."

"Prince of a man."

James patted his lapel pocket. "I've got his note right here."

"That's a pretty story," Letty said. "And you're a world-class con man."

"Call my bluff. Put that gun away and see. I've got a lot of work to do before the sun comes up."

"I'm thinking, if I put this gun down, you'll do one of two things. Shoot me straightaway and bury me on this island. Or take me out into some deep water. Dispose of me there."

"I can certainly understand you thinking the worst. All things considered."

"So then how can you honestly believe I'd ever put this gun down with you still breathing?"

"Because when you think it through, you'll see there's no other way. Maybe I'm lying. You've got three rounds left in that Taurus. You'd kill me. No doubt. If you got really lucky, you might kill one of my other men.

But the third? And the fourth? They'd take you down. And you know this. The thing is, if you shoot me, you'll never find out if I'm lying or telling the truth. 'Cause you'll be dead. In fact, I don't want to alarm you. I don't want you to make any sudden moves. But there's a man standing on the deck right behind you. He's pointing a .357 at your head through one of the panes of glass. And he could've fired sixty seconds ago."

Letty exhaled a long, slow breath.

She hadn't heard any footsteps on the other side of the French doors.

It was a smart play on James's part. Get her to turn her head. Distract her just long enough to raise his weapon and fire.

James was smiling now.

Letty's palms sweating so badly the grip of the revolver was dripping.

"So what do you say, Letty? Doesn't some part of you want to know if I'm actually this good of a liar?"

"Not really."

She squeezed back the hammer.

The moment her finger touched the trigger there was the sound of wood splintering and glass breaking behind her.

The gun fired as someone crashed into her back with devastating force.

She went down hard, crushed under the weight of a man with foie gras on his breath. Footsteps raced down the hallway, the other men pouring into Fitch's bedroom.

She struggled, but it was no use. He had her pinned to the hardwood floor and the gun lay just out of reach.

The man on top of her said, "James, you hit?"

"Just a graze across my shoulder. Damn if that wasn't close, though."

Letty's eyes welled up as she felt him jerk her wrists behind her back and bind them together with a zip tie.

"Quit fighting me, sweetheart," the man whispered into Letty's ear. "It's over. You're done."

16

The noise of the powerboat engines was deafening.

Letty's hair whipped across her face, but she couldn't brush it away with her hands still bound behind her back. James was at the controls and she sat in the bucket seat behind him, next to the man who'd taken her down. He was the oldest of Fitch's security crew. Forty-five or fifty, with shoulder-length hair the color of dishwater.

The sun wasn't up yet, but the first light of dawn had begun to color the eastern sky.

Letty's underwear rippled in the fierce wind.

She shivered.

Waiting for the engines to go silent.

Dreading it.

Of all the ways to die, considering her past, she feared drowning more than anything. Would they tie something around her to weigh her down? Then just throw her over the side?

She would beg for a bullet when the time came.

And if they don't oblige you?

They would *have* to. She'd do whatever it took. She couldn't allow herself to be tossed overboard while still alive. Couldn't spend her last three minutes sinking into the cool, dark sea. Fighting that terrible thirst for oxygen as it swelled up inside her lungs. Meeting the same death her daddy had almost given her.

The panic grew.

She could feel herself beginning to come apart at the seams.

And then . . .

Lights shone in the distance.

James throttled down as they approached the marina.

He guided the boat into an open slip and killed the engines.

He got up and faced Letty.

"Stand up," he told her.

She stood.

The man beside her pulled out a folding knife and cut her wrists free.

James reached into the copilot seat and grabbed a wad of clothes. He handed them to Letty.

"You're letting me go," she said.

James nodded.

"But you let me believe you were going to—"

"You tried to kill me, Ms. Dobesh. My shoulder is still burning. If I were you, I would put those clothes on right now, and get the hell out of my boat."

Letty moved through the lobby of the La Concha Hotel. Despite the wreck she must have looked, the concierge still smiled and nodded as she stumbled past.

She wasn't drunk anymore. Just tired to the point that nothing seemed real. Not the planted palm trees or the chandeliers. Not the eerie quiet of five a.m. Not even her own reflection in the elevator doors as she rode up to her room.

She drifted down the corridor like a vagabond. Old pair of flip-flops. Boxer shorts. A Jimmy Buffett T-shirt from Fitch's closet that had faded into oblivion. She couldn't even think about the last ten hours. They were beyond processing.

Morning was almost here.

She had no money, no idea how she would get back to the mainland.

But one thought kept needling her.

Javier.

The strangest thing was that his betrayal didn't just make her angry. It hurt her, too. It wasn't like he was a friend. She couldn't fathom that Jav was even remotely capable of experiencing the feelings required to maintain a friendship.

And yet . . . it hurt.

They had worked together twice before. Both jobs had been successful. So why had he done this to her?

She shoved her keycard four times into the slot before the light on the door blinked green.

Because he's a psychopath, Letty. He had a need. You filled it. End of story.

She kicked off the flip-flops and staggered toward the bed.

Smelled his exotic cologne a half second before she noticed Javier sitting at the small table by the window.

She brought her hand to her mouth.

The door whisked closed behind her.

In a night of being chased and shot at, none of those horrors could touch the sheer terror of seeing Javier Estrada sitting like a demon in her hotel room.

She stood frozen, wondering if she could get out the door before he stopped her.

"You wouldn't make it," he said. "Please." He motioned to the bed. "I'm sure you're very tired."

Letty sat down on the edge of the mattress and put her face in her hands.

She said, "Oh God."

So many times tonight, she had thought she was going to die and hadn't.

Now this.

After everything.

It was too much.

"What do you want to ask me?" he said.

She made no response.

"Nothing? How about . . . Am I surprised that you are not dead?"

"You son of a bitch." She muttered it under her breath.

"Ask me," he said.

She glared over at him. "Are you surprised I'm not dead."

"I am not," he said.

"Good for you." Her eyes were filling up with tears. "Good. For. You. Why didn't you just let Fitch's men kill me? Wanted to clean up this last little detail yourself?"

"I like you, Letty."

"Has anyone ever told you you're deranged?"

Javier opened a laptop sitting on the table beside a Slimline Glock.

He said, "You may choose to believe I betrayed you. I don't see it that way."

"Really."

He began typing, still watching her out of the corner of his eye.

"There were reasons I couldn't tell you the true nature of the job. It partly had to do with promises I made to our client, Mr. Fitch. But some of it just came down to my faith in you." He stared at her. "Two times before this, we worked together. I've seen you in action. Simply put, you're a survivor. I believed you would survive tonight."

"You had no right to—"

"And yet I did. Next topic. Part of my agreement with Mr. Fitch was that if you survived—if you killed him—his men were not to touch you. I went so far as to promise him that if anyone other than him laid a hand on you, I would kill his men and his sons, too. Was a hand laid upon you?"

"Why didn't you just let me in on this?"

"Because you might've said no. Come over here. I want to show you something."

Letty pushed against her knees and stood.

Already, her legs had gone stiff.

Three feet away, she stopped.

"What?" she asked.

Javier was pointing at the laptop. "Do you see this?"

She leaned over his shoulder, squinting at the screen.

It was an accounts page on a website for the First National Bank of Nassau.

"What's this supposed to be?" Letty asked.

"It's an account I opened for you. Do you see this?"

Javier was pointing at a number.

$1,000,000.00.

"Is that . . ."

"Yes. That's your balance. Do you remember the first thing I asked you when we met back in Atlanta?"

"You asked if I'd risk my life for a million-dollar payday."

"And do you recall—"

"I said yes."

"You said yes. I know I said four million, but I wasn't even paid four for this job. I'm giving you fifty percent. You earned it."

Javier stood.

He stared down at her through those alien blue eyes.

"You know to keep your mouth shut about Fitch."

Letty nodded.

Javier lifted his Glock and jammed it into the back of his waistband. He picked up his leather jacket, slid his arms carefully into the sleeves.

"Why are you giving this to me?" Letty asked.

"Who can say? Maybe we'll work together again."

"You still sold me out."

"You'll get over it. Or you won't."

He walked out.

Letty sat at the table and stared at the computer screen for a long time. She couldn't take her eyes off that number. Light was coming into the sky. The lamps along Duval Street were winking off. She couldn't imagine falling asleep now.

Letty raided the minibar and stocked her purse. Headed out still wearing John Fitch's clothes.

The roof of the hotel was vacant.

The bar closed.

Letty eased down into one of the east-facing deck chairs.

Drank cheap champagne.

Watched the sun lift out of the sea.

Something Jav had said kept banging around inside her head. *It'll buy you enough crystal to kill yourself a thousand times over.* Already she was feeling the itch to score. A pure craving. Is that what lay in store? Three months from now, would she be living out of another motel? Ninety pounds and wasting away? Now that she had enough money to finish the job, would she use until her teeth melted and her brain turned to mush?

Until her heart finally exploded?

She told herself that wasn't going to happen, that she wouldn't lose control again, but she didn't know if she believed it.

The sun climbed.

Soon, there were other people on the roof and the smell of mimosas and Bloody Marys was in the air.

Letty ordered breakfast.

As the morning grew warm, she thought about her son.

In better times—mostly while high—she imagined sweeping back into Jacob's life. Saw them in parks. Parent-teacher conferences. Tucking him into bed at night after a story.

But she didn't want to entertain those fantasies now.

She wasn't fit.

Had nothing to offer him.

She couldn't get the hotel concierge out of her mind. She wondered if he could assist on scoring her a teener and a pipe.

Three times, she started down to the lobby.

Three times, she stopped herself.

It was the memory of the Atlanta motel that kept turning her back. The image of her skeletal reflection in that cracked mirror. The idea of someone someday having to tell her son how his mother had OD'd when he was six years old.

In the afternoon, Letty moved to the other side of the roof. She passed in and out of sleep as the sun dropped. In her waking moments, she tried on three promises to herself, just to see how they fit.

I will set up a trust fund for Jacob with half the money and make it so I can never touch it.

I will check myself into the best rehab program I can find.

If I'm still clean a year from now, then, and only then, will I go to my son.

The next time she woke, there were people all around her and the sun was halfway into the ocean. Letty sat up, came slowly to her feet. She walked over to the edge of the roof.

The people around her were making toasts to the sunset and to each other. Nearby, a woman mentioned a news report concerning the death of John Fitch. The group laughed, someone speculating that the coward had taken his own life.

Letty clutched the railing.

She couldn't escape the idea that it meant something that she'd stayed up here all day. That she'd watched the sun rise, cross the sky, and go back into the sea. She hadn't felt this rested in months, and those promises were looking better and better.

Like something she could own.

Keep.

Maybe even live for.

She knew the feeling might not last.

Knew she might fall down again.

But in this moment, Letty felt like the tallest thing on the island.

A NOTE FROM BLAKE CROUCH ON "SUNSET KEY"

The idea for "Sunset Key" occurred to me in July of 2006 after reading a news story about the death of Kenneth Lay, the disgraced CEO of Enron Corporation. Lay was found guilty of securities fraud in May of 2006, and three and a half months prior to his scheduled sentencing hearing, he died of a heart attack while on vacation in Snowmass, Colorado. He was expecting a twenty-to-thirty-year prison sentence from the judge and would have likely died while incarcerated.

Everything about the nature and timing of Lay's death intrigued me, but even more so, the psychology of the man himself.

Questions started to appear . . .

What were Lay's thoughts during that vacation in Colorado, ostensibly his last days of freedom?

Had his family deserted him or were they staying loyal?

Did he experience remorse or continue to deceive himself when it came to his own guilt?

How hard did he party?

Did he eat amazing food and drink the best wine he could find?

I had a feeling I would eventually write a story featuring such a character, but for the time being, I set the idea aside. It didn't seem like enough to support a novel or a story.

Several years passed.

After I wrote "The Pain of Others," I started brainstorming other potential Letty stories, looking for ways to continue her adventures. I remembered the news reports about Ken Lay and how they had stoked my imagination. And I decided to have Letty visit a man like Lay on his last night of freedom.

Dockery (Letty) and Botto (Javier) share a lighthearted moment on set while filming the pilot.

An important note in terms of thinking about this story vis-à-vis *Good Behavior* the television show: the Javier in "Sunset Key" is not the Javier in *Good Behavior*. The Javier in "Sunset Key" is a true psychopath. He only uses Letty and is fully willing to serve her up to John Fitch with the knowledge that she may be killed. The Javier in *Good Behavior* would never do this. The moment in the show when Javier turns around in Daphne Rochefort's bathroom and sees that Letty has the drop on him is a threshold moment for both of them. From that moment forward, they are intimately connected and will ultimately become each other's saviors.

It was with this concern in mind that we made the decision *not* to include the story of "Sunset Key" in season one of *Good Behavior*. Javier's actions and motivations in this novella didn't track with the character we were setting up for the television show. Moreover, the tone of "Sunset Key" didn't quite fit with the tone of season one. "Sunset Key" veers more into full-on suspense, especially in the latter half of the story with Letty being hunted on the island.

This is not to say that "Sunset Key" will never find its place in *Good Behavior*. If we're lucky enough to get a second season and can find the right way to dramatize "Sunset Key" while keeping within the tone of our show, then I still have hope this novella will have its day on-screen.

GRAB

1

Letty Dobesh reached to freshen up a trucker's coffee from behind the counter. His name was Dale or Dan or Dave—something that started with a *D*. He was a regular. A creepy regular. Came into the diner several times a week. Tall, lanky, never-tipping guy who always wore a red down vest and a John Deere mesh hat.

As Letty filled his mug, he grinned, said, "Know what would look great on you?"

This should be good.

"No, what's that?" she asked without risking eye contact.

"Me."

Now she did meet his eyes. They were small and brown and contained a volatile energy that she recognized—he was a hitter.

"That's beautiful," she said. "You should write Hallmark cards."

The man laughed like he wasn't sure if he'd been insulted.

Her manager called her name from the grill.

"Be there in a sec!" she said.

"No, Letisha. Not in a sec. Now."

She set the pot of coffee back on the warmer and wiped her hands off on her apron. An image blindsided her: Letty at seventy, hobbling around the diner on arthritic feet, hands like claws from a lifetime of this.

The manager was a short, sweaty, unpleasant man. He wore black jeans, black sneakers, and a white oxford shirt with a hideous Scooby-Doo tie. Same outfit always. As she approached, she saw that he held a wire brush in his right hand.

"Good morning, Lloyd."

"Bathrooms. They're disgusting. You were supposed to clean them yesterday."

"Lloyd, I haven't had a chance—"

He shoved the wire brush into her hand. "With a smile."

"I'm smiling on the inside."

Letty scrubbed furiously at a beard of dried shit affixed to the inside of the toilet.

The noise of the jukebox was indistinct through the concrete walls, but a new refrain had taken up residence in her head.

This is my life.

This is my life.

This is my beautiful life.

When the toilet bowl was pristine, she stood looking out of the small window behind the sink. The view was down Ocean Boulevard. Vacation cottages and high-rises all oriented east toward the sea.

There were bars over this small window, and Letty found it fitting. She'd been out of prison now almost ten months, had been clean for half a year, but she hardly felt free.

She was thirty-six years old and she had just worked herself into a sweat cleaning a toilet in a diner.

Bad as prison had been, the walls that had kept her in her cell and in the yard had never screamed *hopelessness* as loud as the barred window in this tiny bathroom. In prison, there was always something to look forward to. The promise of release and, beyond, the possibility of a Life Different.

She felt a sudden, irresistible urge to get high.

You don't do that anymore.

Why?

For Jacob.

She needed to distract herself. If she were back at the halfway house across the sound, she'd either jump in the shower or go for a run. Do something to break that death-spiral thought pattern. Here at work, she could just plug herself into serving the customers. Her therapist, Christian, would tell her to challenge the thought to use. To stop, take a moment, and analyze the error in it.

Where is the error? I feel bad. Getting high will make me feel good. Doesn't get much simpler than that.

But it's not that simple, Letty. Because you won't use once. If you start, you will use until you're broke or dead or back in prison.

A layer of tears fluttered over the surface of her eyes.

There was a knock at the door.

"Just a minute!"

She wiped them away. Smoothed her blue-and-white dress. Pulled herself together.

Lifting the cleaning supplies, she opened the door.

The trucker in the John Deere hat stood in the alcove that accessed the men's and women's restrooms.

"All yours," she said.

He crowded into the doorway.

"Letisha, right?"

"That's right."

"Wanna earn your tip? How's about we go back in there for a spell?"

Letty pushed up against his scrawny, fetid frame. Reaching down, she grabbed his groin and pulled him toward her.

He said, "Oh hell yeah."

Bulge in the vest. Left side. Wallet.

With their lips an inch apart, Letty smiled. She released his manhood and drove her knee straight up into his balls at the same instant her right hand slid inside his vest, fingers diving into the pocket. She snatched the wallet as he keeled over onto the floor. Would've hit him again but Lloyd had appeared at the end of the hallway that opened into the diner, his face twisted up with rage.

"You junkie whore. I didn't have to give a convicted felon a job."

"He was trying to—"

"I don't care. You're fired. Get out."

Letty ripped off her apron and dropped it on the floor beside the moaning trucker, who'd gone fetal in the corner.

She rode the bus into Charleston. Sat in the back going through the trucker's wallet. His name wasn't Dale, Dan, or Dave. It was Donald, and, for a cheapskate, he carried around fat stacks—$420 in cash and three credit cards.

She whipped out her jailbroken iPhone, which she'd retrofitted with a wireless card-reader. Started scanning Donald's Visa, MasterCard, and Amex, dumping sub-$100 deposits into shell accounts.

2

Letty put her hands behind her head and interlaced her fingers. She liked this couch. The leather was always warm. She liked the afternoon view through the open window in the back wall where the two blues met—sky and ocean. The air breezing through was tinged with salt and suntan lotion and the sweet rot of seaweed.

"You got fired?" Christian said. He was seated at his desk several feet away.

"This morning. I'm leaving town tonight. I've already cleared out my room at the halfway house. Won't miss that dump."

"I thought we agreed it would be a good idea for you to hold down that job at least through Christmas."

"I'm done with this place."

"Where will you go?"

"Oregon."

"To see your son?"

"That's the plan."

"Do you feel you're ready for that? Ready to reenter Jacob's life on a permanent, reliable basis?"

"It's the only thing I'm living for, Christian."

"That means this is our last session."

"You've been great. The best part of my time here."

"Are you anxious?"

"About leaving?"

"It's a big deal."

"I know it is."

"How do you feel about it?"

"Ready."

"That's all?"

She stared at the *Thriller*-era Michael Jackson bobblehead on her substance-abuse counselor's desk and said, "Christian, will it make you feel better if I say I'm scared?"

"Only if it's the truth."

"Of course I'm scared."

"Afraid you'll use again?"

"Sure."

"But you know how to fight it now. You're empowered. You know your triggers—external and internal. You know your three steps to ensure sobriety."

"Recognize. Avoid. Cope."

"There you go. And what's your main trigger?"

"Breathing."

"Come on."

"Remembering what a complete failure I am."

"That's not true."

"Convicted felon."

"Letty."

"Meth addict."

"Stop."

"Junkie whore."

"This is counter—"

"And let's not forget—you got Mother of the Year sitting on your couch. Christian, I got triggers everywhere I look."

Christian leaned back in his chair and sighed the way he always did when Letty turned the knife on herself. He was old-school-Hollywood handsome. Cary Grant. Gregory Peck. With his short-sleeved button-down and clip-on tie, he looked like a car salesman. But his eyes invited trust. Kind and wise and sad.

How could they be anything but? Talking all day to losers like me.

"You know if you don't make some kind of peace with yourself, Letty, none of this stuff works."

She let her eyes fall upon a painting on the wall beside Christian's desk, between two framed diplomas. She inevitably found herself staring at it during some point of each weekly session. It was a print of a romantic masterpiece—a man standing in a dark frock coat on the edge of a cliff. His back is to the viewer, and he's gazing out over a barren, fog-swept waste. The landscape looks so hostile and unforgiving it could be another planet.

Christian turned in his swivel chair and glanced up at the wall.

"You like that painting."

"What's it called?"

"*Wanderer above the Sea of Fog.*"

"Nice."

"What do you like about it?"

"I like the man's fear."

"Why do you say he's afraid? You can't even see his face. I think he's exhilarated."

"No, he's afraid. We all are, and this painting says that. It says we're not alone."

"You're not alone, Letty. If you'd take my advice and join a group, you'd see that."

"NA isn't for me."

"Sobriety is a group effort."

"Christian, the only time I never used was when I was working. When I had a job."

"You mean stealing."

"Yeah."

"You still messing around with that?"

She smiled. "You know what they say. You can take the girl out of prison . . ."

"That's just another form of addiction, Letty."

"I get that."

"So what are you saying?"

"I want to stay clean. For me. For my son. But I don't see the world like you do."

"What do you see?"

Her lips curled up into something that could almost be called a smile. She pointed at the painting.

3

Letty left town that evening with her entire life, such as it was, in a suitcase.

Clothes.

A framed photograph of Jacob at four years old, smiling from the top of a slide.

Laptop.

Phone.

And 5K in cash.

With a thermos full of French roast, she drove all night.

Slept at a truck stop in Arkansas the next day.

She got off the interstate where she could and stuck to back roads. Something more therapeutic in driving her Honda Civic beater down a two-lane highway than anything she'd experienced in rehab. A tangible sense of the life before falling behind her like so many miles of faded yellow stripes.

She didn't push herself. Some days she only clocked a hundred miles. Oregon was the final destination, but she made no effort to take a direct course. She meandered and, in the beginning, didn't think about a thing. Just let the landscape scroll. Whole chunks of time when her mind was a bright-blue cloudless sky. When she was so completely out of herself that when she snapped back into the moment, she couldn't even remember driving. She'd be in a new state. On a different road. She wanted more time to pass like that. She lived so rarely in the present, her existence neatly boiled down into two equal parts.

The depression and regret of her past.

The fear of what was to come.

Her two planes of consciousness—or was it "plains"?

And she was driving on the plains of eastern Nebraska on a late-summer afternoon when something like an epiphany struck her. She would always remember the moment, because out the windshield her stretch of prairie was sun-drenched and golden with late light.

When I'm high and when I'm on a job, I'm not plagued by the sadness of the past or the fear of the future.

That's why I use.

Why I steal.

Those are the only times when I live in the moment like a free human being.

She checked into a motel in the eastern desert of New Mexico on her fifth or sixth day. It was after ten p.m., and in the west the sky was getting raked by an electrical storm that was too far out for the sound of its thunder to reach her.

She pulled a chair out onto the concrete balcony.

Sat watching the sky light up, thinking how nice it would be to get high. It wasn't much of a desert town, but she'd driven past a roadhouse on the outskirts. She could take a shower, put on something slinky, head down there, and score. She could almost taste the smoke. Gasoline and plastic and household cleaners and Sharpies and sometimes apples. Oh yes, and nail polish. She hadn't dared to paint her toes in the last six months for fear the odor alone would set her down the bad path.

Challenge the thought to use.

You do it tonight, when you start to come down you'll feel so bad you'll have to go again. And again. Cycle repeats. Then you'll have lived in this motel room for three weeks and eaten nothing but convenience-store food. You'll be frail and sick, right back where you were last fall.

But the urge was still there.

So how do you cope?

If she went back into the room, she knew what would happen. She'd take a shower under the guise of distracting herself. But then she'd get out, suitcase dive for something sexy, and head down to the bar.

So how do you cope?

Stay right where you are.

Do not move.

By midnight, she could hear the thunder and smell the threat of rain in the sky like a closed-up attic. She didn't go inside. Not even when the rain started.

It came down in curtains. The temperature fell. Almost instantly there were pools of standing water in the empty parking lot. The lightning touched the desert a quarter mile away, and the ensuing noise was louder than a shotgun blast at close range.

Still, she didn't move.

Her clothes were drenched and she was shivering.

The storm passed.

Stars appeared.

She could hear the quiet roar of I-40 a mile away.

It was three thirty in the morning.

Struggling to her feet, she pulled open the sliding-glass door and walked into the frigid air-conditioning. She stripped out of her wet clothes and climbed naked into bed. The need was still there, just no longer screaming in her face. Now she pictured it as the embodiment of an emaciated woman, crouched in a corner, whispering madly to herself.

4

She stopped the next afternoon in the red-desert waste of Arizona. It had been twenty-four hours since she'd eaten, something in the ache of an empty stomach that she found useful in fighting the urge to use. If hunger was on her mind, crystal meth wasn't.

But now she was dizzy and light-headed, feared her driving was on the cusp of becoming erratic.

She got off the interstate past Winslow and headed south through a landscape of buttes and exposed rock. A world stripped down to its bones.

She felt so light-headed it was becoming difficult to focus, but a quick glance in the rearview mirror cut through the fog.

The black Tundra that had been trailing her for the last hundred miles, perhaps more, had taken the same exit.

Am I being paranoid because I'm famished?

She pulled into the visitors' center.

Walked up to the drab brick building and paid the admission fee.

Inside, the air-conditioning was set to blizzard.

She pretended to peruse the gift-shop card rack while she stared out the window that overlooked the parking lot.

The driver-side door of the Tundra was open. A black man climbed out.

He wore khaki shorts and a white T-shirt without a logo or slogan.

Letty threaded her way through the tourists and slipped out the exit. She followed the observation path through the desert until she stood on the rim.

The depression was gaping. Nearly a mile across. Five hundred feet deep. She could see people the size of ants on the far side, walking the trail that circled the crater. The heat radiating off the ground was tremendous.

A hole in the ground. Yay.

Turning, she studied the visitors' center—no sign of the black man from the Tundra.

You're imagining things. Go eat something.

◈

She ordered a foot-long veggie sandwich at the Subway in the visitors' center and claimed a booth.

Crazy hungry.

Didn't even come up for air until she was halfway through and nearly choked when she did. Because that man was sitting across from her, smiling. It was a beautiful smile. Broad and bright. But there was something malicious and knowing in it that she couldn't quite put her finger on. Like the man wasn't smiling at her, but rather at something he knew *about* her.

Letty put her sandwich down, wiped her mouth.

"By all means," she said. "Please join me."

The man unwrapped his sandwich—a meatball sub—and dug in.

"You followed me here," Letty said.

He nodded as he chewed.

Through a mouthful, he said, "Picked you up in Gallup."

"What do you mean, 'picked me up'?"

He just smiled.

"There something I can help you with?" she asked.

"Damn, girl. Can I eat my sub first?"

They ate in silence, watching each other. He was thirtysomething, Letty figured, but closing in on forty. Her age, possibly. No trace of stubble. Brown eyes. Movie-star handsome. Shredded.

They finished their sandwiches without a word, and then he washed his down with a long hit of Coke through a straw that sucked his cheeks in.

He said, "Ahhhh. Can't believe they had a Subway. That's just a bonus. You look thoughtful. Lemme guess. You going through all the people you ever wronged, trying to figure out who's come back to settle a score. Yeah?"

Letty made no acknowledgment, but he was right.

"This ain't about none of that," he said. "Ain't here to hurt you. This got nothing to do with anything in your past. All about the future."

That unnerving smile again.

Letty drew in a long breath. Her head was clear now, and she was afraid.

"How'd you find me?"

"Friend of mind in Charleston put a TrimTrac on your ride. Know what that is?" She shook her head. "Little device that lets me track your location using GPS. I heard you was coming west, thought we should meet."

"Why?"

"We'll get to that."

"I have a phone. Just calling would've been less creepy than this by a factor of a hundred."

"I'm more persuasive in person."

"Have we met before?"

"No, but we share a friend."

"Who's that?"

"My man, Jav."

"Javier sent you after me?"

"Not *after* you. *To* you. With a proposal."

"I hope you weren't counting on Javier's name to facilitate whatever the hell you thought was going to happen here."

He reached his hand across the table. "Isaiah."

She didn't take it.

"Damn, that's cold."

"I want you to get your tracking device off my car and leave me alone."

"Why you hatin' when you ain't even heard what—"

"Does Javier want something? Is that what this is about?"

"No, *I* want something."

"I don't understand."

"He recommended you to me."

"For what?"

He grinned. "What do you think? A job."

Letty leaned back against the seat.

"I did some work with Jav last fall," Isaiah said. "He's an interesting—"

"He's a psychopath."

"Be that as it may, he knows a lot of people. I called him last week. Told him about this thing I got going. This bind I'm in. Told him the kind of person, kind of skill set I needed, and he said I had to have you."

"No, I'm done with all that." Even as she said it she tasted the lie. "Do you know why I'm driving across the country, Isaiah?"

"No."

"To see my son."

"For real?"

"For real."

"And what? You ain't seen him in a while?"

She shook her head.

"What happened?"

"Right. I'm going to tell the guy who's been spying on me for the last week about my private affairs."

"You ain't gotta be this way, Letisha. I ain't coming at you with negativity."

She sighed. "What do you want?"

"Javier tells me you the best."

"The best what."

"Best liar he's ever worked with."

"Thanks, I guess."

"And that you got scary-fast hands."

"So."

"So that's exactly what I need."

"I think I already gave you my answer."

"You don't even want the pitch?"

"Nope."

"So you out, huh? Gonna go be Miss Respectable Citizen? Get a nine to five. Pay taxes. All that shit?"

"I'm gonna go be a mother to my son."

Isaiah's eyes didn't exactly soften, but his body language changed. Like someone had let a little air out of the tires.

"That's cool, then. I feel that." He crumpled up his Subway wrapper, slid out of the booth. "Good luck to you, Letisha."

"You too, Isaiah. Hope the score's big and you don't get caught."

His laugh was low, booming. "Never."

She watched him walk out of the restaurant.

Felt suddenly cold.

Alone and empty and void of anything approaching hope.

Here it came, right on cue—the crushing need to use.

Challenge the thought.

When I'm high and when I'm on a job—those are the only times in my life not plagued by the sadness of the past or the fear of the future.

So, tonight you can either be high in some motel room, taking that first step toward running your life into the ground once again.

Or . . .

5

Letty caught Isaiah in the parking lot, crouched down beside her car, prying the tracking device off the undercarriage.

He looked up, grinning.

She said, "I was thinking."

"Yeah?"

"You wanna walk around the crater?"

It was god-awful hot, Letty already sweating.

Isaiah moved slowly along the footpath. They had to keep stopping to let the tour group up ahead gain distance.

"Ever hear of a man named Richter?" he asked.

"What thief hasn't? The rock-star grifter we all want to be. But he's just a myth. Urban legend."

"Actually, he's not."

"You've met him?"

"I'm doing a job with him."

Letty felt a pulse of energy ride up the bones of her legs into her stomach, like it had come from the ground beneath her feet.

"Where's the job?"

"Four and a half hours from where you stand."

She stopped.

Shielded her eyes from the sun as she stared up at him. He was smiling but his eyes were hidden behind a pair of aviator sunglasses.

"Vegas?"

"Fabulous Las Vegas."

She said, "A man I respect very much once told me that of all the jobs in the world, the only one I should never touch was a casino. Said, 'There's all this money floating around waiting for us just to reach up and grab it. Why rob it from the pit of hell?'"

They walked again.

"I'm part of Richter's ten-man crew," Isaiah said.

"What's your superpower?"

"Brute force. Weapons. I was Force Recon back in the day. So the vault in one of the major casinos is having its security system overhauled this coming weekend. We don't know if it's Friday, Saturday, or Sunday."

"I'm not going into any goddamn vault. I'll just tell you that right now."

"Me and you both, sister. Here's the cool part. They don't trust nobody. Not even the security-company personnel. Two hours before the install, they box the cash up and cart it from the vault area into a room in the hotel. Of course, the money is still guarded by its own private army, but at least there's no vault to break it out of."

"And what? Richter has a guy on the inside?"

"Exactly. At some point on Friday, twenty-four to thirty-six hours from now, Richter will get a call or a text from his contact. They'll tell him when the security install is happening and which room in the hotel will be housing all that cash. Richter's plan is ingenious. The crew gains access to the room directly underneath. We go through the ceiling, set up an ambush, and let the money come to us."

"You have blueprints of the hotel?"

"No. Too many variables and possibilities. We'll have to finalize our game plan once we see the room they've chosen."

"Sounds super risky."

"For sure. But the probability of success is much greater than if we had to go through a vault, grab the cash, and fight our way back out through the casino. No amount of money could get me to sign up for that shit."

"I guess I'm just confused. I mean, the idea of working with Richter sounds intriguing. But I'm having a hard time seeing where I fit into all of this. Your plan sounds solid. What do you need me for?"

"Jav said you could be trusted."

"I can."

"You wouldn't be working with Richter."

"I don't understand."

"Richter put the crew together, but he's doing one thing in this whole deal. He's giving us the room number and the time. It's his contact at the hotel. I give him that. But he ain't gonna be anywhere near the hotel room when the half dozen armed guards roll in with the money."

"His contact, his show, right?"

"He's taking half. Other nine of us are splitting the rest. And it's like we should be grateful for the privilege. That sound right to you?"

"Not so much."

"So I'm thinking, sure, Richter's a legend, but fuck him."

"How exactly?"

"I'm running a shadow crew. Brought in Jerrod and Stu, two of my boys from Iraq. We're going to take down this money. Estimate is thirty-eight to forty mil. Split that four ways, including you, we're talking possibly seven zeros apiece. You know what I call that?"

"No, what do you call that?"

"I call that you-ain't-gotta-do-shit-ever-again money. I call that living-right-for-the-rest-of-your-life money. Don't tell me some part of you hasn't always dreamed of robbing a casino."

She was starting to see it—her place in this madness.

They had walked half a mile, and she was dripping with sweat. She looked back at the visitors' center.

"Richter's phone," she said. "You want me to grab it. That's why you want me, right?"

Isaiah grinned. "Among other things."

"What other things?"

"Whatever we need. But nothing you can't handle. And if you ain't down for that, I'm happy to pay you a flat rate for the grab. But if you want to be in on the split, you see this thing through to the end."

"I don't do jobs that require guns," she said. "Not for any amount of money."

"Well, I guess it's your lucky day."

"No guns? Seriously?"

"No guns for the takedown. Too noisy. Too messy. But if things turn to shit after, I make no promises. If you need to think it over, I can give you one hour. But the clock is ticking."

"No."

"No?"

"I don't need to think it over."

6

Letty rolled down Las Vegas Boulevard at sunset, the Strip already aglow.

It had been five years since her last visit, and she was happy to see that everything about this city still got under her skin in the best kind of way. Where most people saw absurdity and flash, she saw art and life and possibility. There was the Venetian, lit up like a white angel. The MGM Grand the color of money or the guy at the blackjack table losing his shirt while everyone around him wins.

She loved the universal hustle.

The bellboys, the strippers, the hookers, the dealers, the doormen, the bartenders.

Everyone angling.

She could live here.

Isaiah had checked her into a Prestige Suite at the Palazzo. After a week of Motel 6s and worse, this elevation into luxury made her exuberant.

She ordered up room service, then headed downstairs to find an outfit for the evening with the envelope of hundos that Isaiah had provided as a starting expense account.

She bought a dress at Chloé.

Pumps at Christian Louboutin.

Had a makeover at a salon called Fresh.

By ten o'clock she looked like a completely different creature. The seven-day accumulation of road grunge gone. She stood at the window in the living room of her suite, looking down at the traffic moving along Sands Avenue twenty-eight floors below. Across the street, she had a perfect view of their ultimate target.

The sleek curve of the Wynn.

But tonight wasn't about money or a vault.

Tonight was all on her.

Richter and his crew would be at Tryst at eleven p.m.

A knock at her door pulled her away from the window.

Through the peephole, she saw a bellboy.

Opened the door.

"I have a package for you, ma'am."

She took the small box and gave him a five-spot.

Letty carried it into the kitchen. It resembled an expensive gift box. Simple. Elegant. Gold paper. Her phone rang as she tugged off the white ribbon and tore at the wrapping paper.

"Hello?"

"Get my package?"

"You really shouldn't have."

She lifted the top off the box.

A black iPhone and a photograph.

The photo was a headshot of a white man with a shaven head and a few days' worth of stubble darkening his jawline. For some reason the smooth head and intense eyes reminded Letty of a thug in a European heist flick. Otherwise, he was unremarkable. Nothing like how she'd imagined the legend. Then again, maybe that was the point.

Isaiah said, "I'll need access to Richter's phone for one hour. This is his replacement."

"Does it work?"

"No. It was impossible for Mark to replicate his contact list, apps, texts, call history. Safer play to swap it for a nonfunctioning phone. It'll power up and display a black screen. What I'm asking isn't easy. I need you to swap his current phone out for this one. Then you're going to have to hand off his phone to my contact at the club. He'll find you, so don't worry about that. Then you have to entertain Richter for an hour while my guy builds the clone. Then you have to switch his real phone back for the fake."

She said, "What if he freaks when his phone doesn't work?"

"If he's into you, maybe he doesn't even think about his phone for an hour."

"This is a tall order," she said. "Just so you know."

"Tall orders come with big paydays. You got this, Letisha?"

"Yeah. And by the way, it's Letty. I go by Letty."

"Aiight. Since we turning into homies, I go by Ize."

"See you in the club, Ize."

7

Even at ten thirty, the line to get into Tryst was ridiculous. Letty was pretty sure she looked fabulous, but in the back of her mind, her age kept popping. Fifteen years older than almost everyone around. She didn't look thirty-six, at least not tonight. Could've possibly passed for something that started with a two depending on the lighting, but still . . .

The group ahead of her consisted of two couples.

One of the guys was trying to talk to a doorman in black slacks and a muscle T with the cold eyes of an assassin. A man who had heard every plea to get inside. He was flipping pages on a clipboard and shaking his head.

"I don't see you on anybody's guest list. And just to be straight up with you, there's no way you're going inside wearing sandals and shorts."

"Are you kidding me?"

"Do I look like I'm kidding you? Go put on some adult clothes and try again."

"This is bullshit."

The doorman looked past the group, met eyes with Letty.

She pushed her way through to the velvet rope.

"How's your night going?" she asked.

"No complaints. What's your name?"

"I'm not on anybody's guest list."

"We're pretty full tonight."

"How about I just give you a hundred bucks?"

She already had it in her hand. The doorman looked down, took it, opened the velvet rope.

She tried not to let it eat at her as she moved through the lounge area toward the entrance, the house music beginning to build. She'd had to slide a bribe to get in. Couldn't deny it. It stung.

The lounge was a spread of reserved tables and clusters of beautiful people.

She opened her purse, checked her phone.

A new text from Isaiah: `north patio by the waterfall`

She paid her cover charge and entered the club.

The place was mobbed and loud beyond any level of pleasure she could conceive of. Straight on, the DJ booth was manned by a clean-cut white kid whose day job you would never suspect outside these walls. Behind it, a waterfall crashed into a lake. Paths branched off the dance floor, one leading toward the main bar, the other to what she guessed was a VIP lounge.

The decor and vibe felt seedy, dark, and elegant all at once.

The strobe was disorienting, the heat on the dance floor massive.

As she skirted through, two men caught her eyes and tried to lure her in.

The air redolent of alcohol, cologne, sweat.

She fought her way to the doors leading out onto the north patio.

Despite it being summertime in the desert, it was cooler outside the crush of pheromones.

The pool teemed with schools of bikini-clad women and ripped men.

The stimulation dizzying.

She wanted a drink. A hit of crystal.

It was the most beautiful nightclub she'd ever seen, and to be here carefree and high would have been exhilarating.

To be here on a job, she had to admit, was a close second.

Even outside, there was no place to sit. Every table either filled or reserved.

She spotted Isaiah standing near a table in the far corner, tucked in beside the waterfall. He was laughing and he looked good—designer blue jeans, Red Wing boots, black T under a green velvet bomber jacket. He stood with four other men, far outnumbered by the entourage of women surrounding them.

It took Letty several minutes to make her way through the crowd to the outskirts of Isaiah's table.

She stood alone.

So much movement, so much conversation all around her.

Lanterns hung from the trees and she could just hear the white noise of the falling water.

Nine hours ago, she'd been talking to Isaiah at the crater.

Seemed like years ago.

A trainwreck of a thought barreled through her mind.

There are so many women here more beautiful than you. Richter is surrounded by them. Why would he give you the time of day? Why should he? You look out of place here. You had to pay extra just to get inside—

Stop. Maybe challenging the thought works on a job, too?

Quit being insecure.

This isn't the hardest thing you've ever done.

You know how to make people like you.

I need a drink.

No you don't.

Yes I do.

She let the stimulation overwhelm her.

The smell of champagne like spring in the air.

The starless Vegas sky.

The voluptuous architecture of the Wynn.

The bright blue of the pool and the yellow glow behind the ninety-foot waterfall.

The red heat inside the club.

The infectious groove as the DJ remixed a song she liked—Cowboy Junkies covering "Ooh Las Vegas."

Everyone around her was moving. She let her hips begin to sway. Everyone was here to have fun and so was she. So was Richter.

She *had* this.

Letty moved closer to their table.

There.

Talking to one of the orbiting women who looked just bimbo enough to possibly be an escort.

Richter was shorter than she'd imagined. Barely five-ten. He wasn't handsome, just put together nicely. Retro glasses. A short-sleeved button-down that seemed to shimmer. No belt. Shiny black wingtips. No jacket.

In that case, she'd be mining the front pockets of his slacks. Back pocket would be better. Cargo-pants pockets ideal. But front pocket was workable, and his pants didn't look too tight. In fact, it was more in her comfort zone than a grab from an inner jacket pocket. A pants pocket was a pocket. What you saw was what you got, with tightness being the only variable. An inner jacket pocket that you couldn't see was full of surprises. Like zippers. Snaps. Buttons. All manner of things to snag probing fingers.

She could feel her adrenaline begin to spike as she approached. She drew within range of Richter and the bimbo. The woman stood on legs that looked too insubstantial to support her top half.

Richter was staring at her with a glazed look that Letty hoped was boredom.

She inched closer.

Overheard the bimbo shouting, "Yah, I've been out here about a year and a half. It's pretty fun, you know. Lots to do. Sometimes, I wake up and it's like, I live in Vegas, right? Like, oh my God!"

Letty looked up at Richter.

Eye contact.

He said, "And what's this? Another fly come to suck off our bottle service?"

He turned away from both women, called out, "Gentlemen, let's roll."

Letty shoved down the flush of rage.

Do not let him leave.

But she couldn't think of a single play to stop this from happening.

Bimbo said, "Asshole," and stormed off.

Richter and the rest of his crew headed out, with Isaiah bringing up the rear.

He didn't even look at her.

8

Letty's feet were killing her. She eased down into one of the chairs at the empty table.

Steaming.

In shock.

She'd choked.

Her first job since last Christmas, and she'd blown it.

A promoter materialized—cute brunette with chopped hair. Amazing dress. Name tag read "Jessica."

She smiled at Letty and knelt down so she didn't have to shout.

"Hi, what's your name?"

Letty said, "Gidget."

"Well, Gidget, this is actually a reserved table. I have a group I need to put here."

Screams from the next table over drew Letty's attention. Looked like a bachelorette party unfolding. Pure, smashed joy.

Letty slid back into her pumps, struggled onto her feet.

"All yours."

Letty headed back toward the dance floor. Just wanting to get out of the noise, out of the movement.

Inside it was, impossibly, more crowded than before.

A wall of bodies.

The music ear-rupturing.

The bass heart-stopping.

She moved along the perimeter.

A group of three guys at a table called out to her with Boston accents. They were working their way through a 1.75-liter bottle of Jack and they reeked of desperation. Any other night, she'd have had a drink and grabbed their wallets.

It took her five minutes to push through the crowd and past the entrance into the front lounge.

The barrage of self-destructive thoughts firing away.

You've lost it.

You're washed up.

Then she was passing a line of nightclub hopefuls that snaked through the lobby of the Wynn.

Then she was outside, sucking down gulps of exhaust-tinged desert air.

She kicked off her shoes and carried them.

Her head swirling.

She felt her phone vibrate. Opened her purse.

A text from Isaiah: `wtf was that?`

Good question.

She hit him back: `location?`

He answered: `stand down see u tomorrow`

She went up to her room, but she couldn't calm down. Couldn't stand the thought of lying in bed playing her epic fail over and over again.

She needed to score.
Challenge the thought.
I need to get high.
Challenge the thought. Think about your son. Think about—
I need to get high.

She wound up at the Zebra Lounge, a bar in her hotel with tons of seating upholstered in zebra print. Onstage, dueling pianists played something fast and obnoxious.

She sat at the bar. Hadn't had a drink since starting rehab in Charleston, and she wanted to fall off the wagon with something big and noisy.

While the bartender made her Long Island Iced Tea, she studied him, trying to get a read on whether he would further her ultimate ambitions for the evening.

He was twenty-three or twenty-four. Smooth-shaven. Cropped hair. Lifted weights for sure. No tats that she could see, although he wore a long-sleeved black button-down, which didn't reveal much.

He set her drink in front of her, said, "Seventeen dollars. Start a tab?"

"Sure, put it on my room." She gave him the number. "What's your name, by the way?"

"Darren."

"Darren, if I wanted to get my hands on something a little stronger than booze, would you be able to point me in the right direction?"

She could see in his eyes that he got asked this *all the time.*

"Talk to Jay at Japonais in the Mirage. He's working tonight."

"Appreciate that."

He left her to her drink.

It was strong and very good.

Yes, the night had blown, up to this moment, but she was about to turn it around.

Letty leaned over her drink and sucked the rest of it down.

The liquor hit her gut in a burst of beautiful heat.

9

Letty crossed the boulevard.

The Strip at midnight sleepless and blinking and radiating a nervous energy that filled her junkie soul with the closest thing to joy she could ever hope to know.

Even at this hour, too much traffic creeping between the median of palm trees.

Almost everyone she passed was lit up.

Hell, she was, too.

It felt good to be outside again, walking and buzzed and the Mojave air skirting over her shoulders, between her knees.

Surreal to be in the midst of all this stimulation and to know that twenty miles in any direction would put you in abject emptiness.

Between Treasure Island and the Mirage, a small black man wailed on a harmonica. Playing for tips, but no one was tipping. Letty dropped a twenty into the Panama Jack hat lying upturned on the sidewalk beside him.

He looked up.

"Bless you. Bless you."

Huge, milky cataracts covered his eyes, but he stared right at her. His smile both penetrating and disarming.

Letty moved on.

"You don't have to give up!" he called after her. "I hope you know that!"

She quickened her pace.

The giant marquee on the Mirage blazed down like a midnight sun.

The volcano in front of the casino erupted.

A crowd snapped photos with their phones.

Letty cruised through the tropical landscaping into the hotel.

An adult fantasy world.

The atrium filled with vegetation.

A massive aquarium behind the front desk.

It took her five minutes to find the bar, another ten once she was seated before the rail of a man with long, curly hair finally came over.

She said to him, "Are you Jay?"

"Yeah, why?"

"I'd like a Floating Orchid and some advice."

"Who sent you?"

"Darren from the Zebra Bar."

She watched him make something out of vodka, Cointreau, and the juice of a pear and a lemon.

He set it in front of her, and she gave him a fifty-dollar bill, said, "Keep it."

Jay looked like Joey Ramone circa the Carter administration. He put his elbows on the bar, leaned toward her, said, "What are you looking for?"

"Crystal."

He gave her a corner in North Las Vegas, a first name, and a description of the dealer.

She never touched her drink.

As she was heading down the sidewalk, on the lookout for a cab, the trigger sweats kicked in. Like beads of anticipation rolling down the insides of her legs. That wasted woman Letty pictured as her need now screaming in her ear, wild-eyed, ebullient for the coming fix.

Challenge the thought—

I have. The thought kicked my ass.

Somewhere between the Mirage and Caesars Palace, the sound of youthful voices pulled her attention away from the taxi search.

Up ahead, a group of Mexican kids were singing their hearts out in Spanish.

Letty didn't know the words, but she recognized the tune.

"Sublime gracia."

"Amazing Grace."

It stopped her in her tracks. Something about the contrast—these little voices surrounded by all this decadence.

Before she knew it, she was lost in the spectacle.

They finished the song and moved on.

Behind them stood a small church—utterly out of place on the Strip.

There were lights on inside, and she could hear a man's voice pushing over the din of boulevard traffic.

She climbed the stone steps toward the double doors.

Shrine of the Most Holy Redeemer.

Some mysterious gravity drawing her out of the commotion of late-night Vegas.

She slunk in, took a seat in the back pew.

The sanctuary was brightly lit. It smelled of coffee.

There was a simple crucifix behind the altar. A statue of the Madonna. A statue of Christ holding a child.

At the podium, the harmonica man spoke to the group of twenty or thirty people.

"I'm here to tell you that sobriety ain't easy. But it is simple. If someone told a cancer patient all you had to do was follow these simple steps. Go to meetings. Help others. That you'd get well. You'd do whatever you needed to do to save your lily-white behinds.

"I lost my wife, Irene, last winter. My boy, Lazlo, he dyin' of hepatitis in prison. These are not easy things."

The man cut loose a big, beaming smile.

"But I suit up and show up. See, I have true freedom. Freedom of self. Freedom of self-will. It starts with asking for help. Then you realize you aren't terminally unique. You're one of us. And you never have to be alone again."

Maybe she'd been primed by "Sublime gracia," by the sheer serendipity of finding this church on the Strip, of all places, in a moment of weakness, but Letty felt something like a tiny crack opening in the hardened core of her being. Before she could second-guess or talk herself out of it, she woke her iPhone and deleted the details of her tweak hookup.

The harmonica player said, "Anybody else got something to say? Something to share? You ain't gotta be eloquent. Ain't gotta talk for long. You just gotta be real."

Letty got up.

Her heart beating out of her chest.

She walked down the aisle toward Harmonica Man.

Then he was sitting and she was standing.

It had happened so fast.

What are you doing?

She put her hands on the podium.

The fluorescent lights humming above her.

The muted noise of traffic bleeding through the walls.

She looked out at all the faces.

Young.

Old.

Rich.

Poor.

Black.

White.

Cholo.

Card dealers just off shift.

Cocktail waitresses.

Doormen.

Drivers.

Tourists.

Addiction.

The great equalizer.

"I'm Letisha," she said.

The room responded, "Hello, Letisha."

"I'm an addict," she said. "Alcoholic. Junkie. I was on my way to score when I passed this church. Something pulled me in. I don't know what. I've hurt a lot of people in my life." She felt a storm of grief gathering, but she fought her way through it. "My ex-husband. Myself. My . . . my son.

"I didn't want to come to a meeting. I don't know what I thought. If it was pride. Or fear. But I'm looking out at all of you, and I understand I'm not bigger than crystal and booze. They own my soul forever. But I think maybe we all are bigger. Maybe I see that now. I hope I do. I think I can gain strength from you. I hope one day that you can gain strength from me. That's all I have to say."

Outside on the stone steps, she sat down and wept like she hadn't in years. Not since a court had terminated her parental rights.

After a long time, she struggled onto her feet.

She wasn't even thinking about finding a cab to take her to North Las Vegas.

Across the boulevard, her hotel loomed.

She started walking.

10

Next morning, Letty cabbed out to an IHOP in the xeriscaped burbs, several miles west of the glitz of the Strip.

The emotion of the previous night still clung.

She felt different. Better. New.

Suit up and show up.

Isaiah was waiting for her.

Coffee and a newspaper.

He set the paper aside as she slid into the booth.

The waitress brought coffee.

When she was gone, he said, "There's no way you're this badass Jav told me about."

"I'm sorry."

"You're sorry? For what? Costing me a shit-ton of money? Don't worry about it. Ain't nothing. S'all good."

"The club was a bad approach," she said. "You guys were getting mobbed by women. Richter was done with that scene before I ever showed up."

"So what? You let *his* mood affect your performance? You're amateur, you know that?"

"I had a bad night. It had been a long time since—"

"Oh, so you out of practice? That's the excuse?"

"You ever have a bad night, Ize?"

"No, that's not an option for professionals."

"I can still do this."

"You out your mind? Think I'm gonna let you take another crack at fucking this up? Last night was it, aiight? Anytime today, Richter gets the call. I could get a text from him right now. Then it's showtime. We done. Game over."

Letty leaned back in the booth. Held her hand to the coffee mug until her skin burned.

"What's he doing today?" she asked. "Richter."

"Just chillin'. Waiting for that magic call."

"And where exactly is he just chillin'?"

"Pool at the Wynn."

The waitress returned. "You folks ready to order?"

Letty was already scooting out.

Isaiah said, "Where you going?"

She smiled. "To buy a bikini."

The Wynn pool was wall-to-wall, even at ten thirty a.m., the crowd combating hangovers with mimosas, Bloody Marys, champagne cocktails.

She circled twice before spotting him.

Tucked away in a row of private cabanas.

Anonymous beyond the bikinis, board shorts, and occasional banana hammock.

Richter was oiled and soaking up the sun, a thin gold chain glittering in his chest hair, eyes hidden behind sunglasses. Two other men she recognized from the nightclub sunbathed beside him.

She walked to the bar at the far end and ordered three champagne cocktails. The bartender didn't want to lend her a tray. A twenty-spot sealed the deal.

It was a hike back to Richter's cabana. Letty could feel the scorching heat of the white pavement coming through the soles of her bejeweled Escada flip-flops. The bikini wasn't really her style—a skirt-bottomed black-and-white-striped two-piece. Nor was it an exact match for the pool's cocktail-waitress swimwear. But it was close.

She moved away from the main pool, up the walkway leading to the private cabanas. On full alert now. In all likelihood, there was a personal waiter assigned to each cabana.

She approached a man in white board shorts and an open shirt.

One of the waiters?

She smiled, but he passed without acknowledgment.

Richter's cabana stood at the end.

Reggae music sweetened the air.

She veered toward it and slowed her pace, squinting through her Jimmy Choo shades to absorb every detail.

Three men. Chairs side by side in the sun. Too scaldingly bright to see into the cabana, but she couldn't imagine Richter's phone would be inside. He was waiting on a critical call. The phone would be close. Within reach.

She stopped at the foot of the trio of beach chairs and smiled down at Richter and his men. Richter was in the middle. The one on the left was a hairy beast of a man with the fat-over-muscle build of someone who'd earned their conditioning from life experience, not a gym bike. Someone who possessed the brute core strength to physically break you. The man on the right was younger and leaner, but still carried plenty of brawn. It squared with Isaiah's story—these weren't techie savants hired to pull a sophisticated vault break. Richter was lining up big scary men to storm a hotel room and take down an army of casino thugs by force.

They all wore sunglasses, and she couldn't tell if they had noticed her yet.

Letty cleared her throat.

Richter tugged out his earbuds.

He's listening to music. Which means his phone is in his pocket, headphones plugged in. Extra challenge points.

He said, "We didn't order those."

"Gentlemen, these are compliments of the Wynn."

Letty took a step forward, letting the front of her left flip-flop snag on a lip in the pavement.

She went down hard.

The tray dumped onto Richter's chair.

Two of the champagne flutes shattered against the concrete.

The third splashed across Richter's lap.

He jumped up and swore.

Letty struggled to sit up.

She'd nailed it. Bloody knee and everything. She clutched it and made a whimpering sound.

"Oh my God. Oh my God, I am so sorry."

She glanced up at Richter. He was staring down at her. Where she'd expected rage, she found concern.

"You all right?" he asked.

"I hurt my knee."

"Yeah, that looks nasty."

His phone. He was holding it now.

She reached up to him with both hands.

Put it down. Put it down.

He hesitated for a split second and then dropped his phone on the chair cushion.

"Let's get you up out of this glass."

"They're gonna fire me," Letty said as he pulled her onto her feet.

"Nobody's getting fired."

Blood ran down her leg and she could feel a shard of glass embedded in her skin. She staggered back and collapsed onto the end of Richter's chair. His phone lay right beside her, specked with beads of champagne cocktail.

"Does it feel like you cracked anything?" Richter asked.

All three men knelt in front of her, studying her knee.

"I don't think so," she said as she slipped the dummy iPhone out of her bikini bottoms.

"I'm just worried if my boss sees this, she'll fire me. I'm already on probation."

Dropped it beside Richter's phone.

Tugged the earbuds out of his phone's jack—

"She's a total bitch."

—plugged them into the dummy.

Richter said, "Bill, would you get her a towel, please?"

She palmed his phone, slid it back into her briefs.

As the large, hairy man hustled into the cabana, Letty stood up.

"What's your name?" Richter asked.

"Selena."

"You're not going to get into any trouble over this, okay? I'm not going to let that happen, Selena."

"I just feel bad I ruined your day."

"You didn't ruin anybody's day. Simple accident."

Bill returned with a towel.

Letty wiped the blood off her leg and wrapped it around her waist.

"I better go get washed up," she said. "I'll send someone to clean this mess. Again . . . I'm real sorry."

"Forget it."

And then she was walking away from the cabana, the piece of glass tingling in her knee—a sharp, bright sting—but she didn't care. Richter's phone jostled against her ass and this moment was the closest thing to being high that she'd felt in months.

11

Letty saw him standing under an overhang of trees in the lobby of the Wynn. He barely looked old enough to be in college. Black Chuck Taylors, baggy jean shorts, a gray Billabong hoodie.

She pulled Richter's phone out of her bikini and walked up to him. He smelled like pot, his eyes red with a stoner sheen.

"Mark?"

"Letty?"

She handed him Richter's phone, said, "I'm in 812. How long?"

"One hour."

"I need you to bust a move. This thing is only halfway done."

Riding up in the elevator, she called Isaiah.

"I got it," she said. "You heading over?"

"On my way."

"Let me know how it goes. I'll be back down as soon as Mark drops off the phone."

"It went well?"

"Yeah. But I'm concerned their waiter will interfere, freak everyone out when he hears what happened."

"I'll damage-control."

"See you soon."

This room was smaller but nicer than the one at the Palazzo. She turned on the news and went into the bathroom. Dug out the piece of glass and cleaned up her knee.

She sat on the end of the bed and stared at the plasma screen but her mind was elsewhere.

Thirty minutes in, she got a text from Isaiah: `trouble`

She texted back: ?

`real waiter showed`
`run interference`
`tryin`

Fifty-five minutes after the handoff, there was a knock on her door.

Through the peephole—Mark standing in the hallway, beaming and proud.

She let him in.

"It worked?" she asked.

"Like a mofo."

◈

Letty moved toward the cabanas. Isaiah stood with Richter's crew and a twentysomething man in white shorts and an open shirt. The real waiter.

Her phone vibrated.

Isaiah: `do not approach`

She turned away just as Richter emerged from the cabana. Ducked behind a potted cypress and watched him storm past with his goons in tow.

She fell in after Isaiah, trailing him by five feet, typing out a text as she walked.

`behind you`

Up ahead, she could see Richter holding the dummy iPhone. He had ripped off the bumper case and was fumbling with it.

Bill said, "You can't just take the battery out of an iPhone. You have to go to an Apple Store."

The other guy said, "Or just YouTube it. I'm sure it can be done."

Isaiah pulled out his phone.

He didn't look back. Just started texting.

```
he's freaking
this is getting ready to explode
```

She tapped out: where's he going?

He responded: his room

A congestion of sunbathers had slowed the procession. Letty blasted ahead, past Isaiah, elbowing her way through the masses.

She hit the hotel entrance fifteen seconds before Richter and his group.

Rushed ahead into the expansive, chiming casino.

He'd have to pass through on his way to the tower elevators.

She glanced back, saw Richter and his men entering.

Pushed on, faster, down a red-carpeted corridor between miles of slot machines. The way the overhead lighting struck the marble made it look like gold.

This was it.

Make the switch now or forget it.

From Richter's perspective, his phone was malfunctioning. He was waiting on a call or a text worth millions. If he hadn't already, he'd call his contact, give him a new way to reach him. And that would be that.

Letty stopped at the perimeter of a field of table games.

Craps, blackjack, Pai Gow, Big Six.

It reeked of cigarette smoke, the air hazy with it, especially under the constellation of hanging globe lamps that ranged as far as she could see.

A herd of cocktail waitresses on the prowl.

Richter was coming.

She could feel her phone vibrating, Isaiah no doubt wondering what the hell she was doing.

One chance.

She'd made a thousand grabs in her lifetime, but nothing like this.

Nothing approaching stakes on this order of magnitude.

Thirty feet away now.

The group moving quickly. Richter out in front, flanked by the original thugs from the cabana, Isaiah bringing up the rear.

Her phone vibrated again.

Ize's new text: `forget about it`

She reached into her purse and traded her phone for Richter's.

Heart beginning to thump. Lines of sweat running over the strings of her bikini top.

Richter wasn't holding his phone. He'd put on a T-shirt and sandals, and she could see the outline of the dummy phone swinging in the left pocket of his trunks.

The pocket looked deep as hell. Jaws. Like it could swallow her arm up to her elbow.

Game on.

She thought about her father.

The tears flowed.

She peeled away from the tables.

Felt the heat from a galaxy of cameras staring down at her. Casino certainly wasn't the ideal setting for this, but oh well.

She started toward them.

Pictured it happening.

Perfect execution.

Twenty feet away.

Richter's sunglasses were tilted up across the bald dome of his head and he looked angry.

Her phone vibrated in her purse.

She ignored it.

Ten feet.

She switched Richter's phone into her right hand, clutched it between her first and second finger, powered it on.

Stared at the red carpeting, tears running fast down her cheeks now. Beginning to tap into that well of emotion that underlay her soul like an aquifer.

Looked up as she bumped into Richter.

He stopped. Studied her through hard hazel eyes.

They stood inches apart.

As she dipped her right hand into his left pocket, she said, "I hope you're happy."

Fighting to keep her fingers from touching his leg.

"What are you talking about?"

"You lied to me."

There. The dummy iPhone.

All at the same instant, she

—jabbed a finger into his chest

—lifted the dummy iPhone with her thumb and pinkie

—let Richter's iPhone slide gently out of her grasp

—said, "You told me I wouldn't—"

Even the best pickpockets in the world rushed the ending. Once your fingers touched the goods, the impulse to grab it and get to safety became overpowering.

She took it nice and slow.

Because she *had* this.

"—get into any trouble."

"I—"

"They fired me."

The phone was clear of his pocket.

She jabbed a finger into his chest again, said, "I have a young daughter. Rent to pay."

Slipped it into her purse.

"What am I supposed to do? Huh?"

Now she crossed her arms and glared at him and let the tears stream down her face.

A thought flashed—*What if he doesn't try his phone again?*

Richter said, "I don't have time for this," and started to move on.

She blocked his way. "You're mad because I spilled champagne on you? Sorry. It was an accident."

The rage came over him almost without warning.

"Your little accident ruined my phone."

"It didn't touch your phone."

Pull it out. Show me I'm wrong. Do it, you cocksucker. Do it.

He thrust his hand into his pocket, dug out his iPhone.

She grabbed it from him, pressed the sleep/wake button, held it up so he could see. His eyes went wide when the screen brightened.

"Looks fine to me."

"Thirty seconds ago, it wasn't—"

She shoved it into his chest, said, "Asshole," and pushed her way between the thugs.

She stared at Isaiah as she moved past.

Said, "What are you looking at?"

And winked.

12

Ten minutes later, Letty let Isaiah into her room at the Wynn.

"I take back everything I said about you," he said. "That grab-and-switch was off the chain. You got ninja skills."

"Richter's okay now? I was worried he'd get another phone or—"

"Nah, he's cool. We all cool." Isaiah moved past her. "What up, Mark?" They bumped fists.

"We're in biz," Mark said. "Come check it."

Letty followed them over to the bed, where Mark had a laptop open. He lifted a white iPhone off the comforter, tossed it to Isaiah.

"That's a perfect clone of Richter's phone. Has all his voice mails, text history, contacts, data usage, apps. More importantly, every call or text that comes to Richter will first hit us. We'll have the option to intercept, pass along, or kill it. You'll see the incoming texts and calls on that phone. I'll see them on my laptop. If it's okay with you, I'll just set up my base of operations here."

"Most definitely," Isaiah said. "And I want you to study his contact list. We gotta let a few calls through so he doesn't suspect anything, but nothing from a Vegas area code. No texts we don't understand. Nothing that looks like code."

"Is Richter's contact from the casino going to call or text?" Letty asked. "Or do we even know?"

"No idea."

Mark said, "I'll scan through his text history and see if I can pin down any promising leads."

Isaiah grabbed one of the walkie-talkies off the dresser and slipped in an earpiece.

"We stay in constant communication until that magic text or call comes."

"You got it," Mark said.

"If a call comes in, we talk it through. Any uncertainty, it doesn't go to Richter."

"Agreed. And what if a Vegas phone number shows up? Or worse, a private number?"

"Then we roll the dice and I answer. I got Richter's voice down cold just in case."

Isaiah pocketed the white iPhone and grinned at Letty.

"You done good, girl."

"Glad it worked out."

"You heading back to the Palazzo?"

"That's the plan."

"I'll walk you out."

In the hallway, Isaiah stopped her.

"My suggestion—go back to your room, get some sleep. This shit may go down in the wee hours."

"Rest of your crew's in town?"

"Everybody's on standby. Soon as we know the room number, we're ready to get it on. What's wrong?"

"Nothing."

"You want out now, that's cool. I'll peel off two-fifty for your work and you can go on your merry way. No more risk."

Tempting.

But the truth was, she didn't want the job to end.

"I told you I'd see it through, Ize."

"That's my girl."

"What about Mark. Is he—"

"Work for hire. He's also our driver. He knows enough to do his job, but no more. You, me, Jerrod, and Stu. That's the only way this money splits."

She started walking toward the elevators.

He called out after her, "Get on your game face, girl!"

Letty moved through the lobby of the Palazzo, under a glass dome and past a two-story fountain.

The high from stealing Richter's phone was fading.

Fear rushing in to take its place.

She hadn't really thought beyond the initial grab. Hadn't begun to come to terms with the concept of Isaiah and his buddies taking down a heavily armed casino-security team. Much less *her* place in that equation.

Up ahead, a man sat on a bench, his face buried in his hands.

It was the hair she recognized—perfectly trimmed brown on the cusp of turning silver. A part she'd recognize anywhere.

She stopped and said, "Christian?"

Her therapist looked up, cologned with booze, eyes red and swollen with tears. He wore a wrinkled sports jacket and khaki slacks that looked like they'd been slept in.

"Letty?" he said.

"What are you doing here?" she asked.

He wiped his eyes, said, "Not having one of my better days on this planet."

"Let me help you up to your room."

"You ever notice you can't open a window in a hotel room? Why is that? How did they know I wanted to jump?"

"Are serious with that? You don't want to jump, Christian. Come on." She grabbed his arm. "Let's get you upstairs. They're gonna throw you out if you stay down here in this condition."

She pulled him onto his feet.

They stumbled toward the elevators.

"You don't have to do this," Christian said. "Nobody is nice like this anymore."

They rode up to the thirty-first floor, just the two of them in the car.

He laughed bitterly. "My first thought was black," he said. "All the way driving out here, it was always going to be black."

"What are you talking about?"

"But I changed my mind at the last minute. Went with red. And then, of course, it hit on black."

"I don't under—"

"I lost a little money this morning."

"On roulette?"

"Red or black. Red or black. Red or black."

"How much did you lose?"

"Everything."

"You bet your life savings?"

"Before I came here, I sold my house. Cashed out my portfolio. Emptied my bank accounts. Two hundred and eighty-five thousand dollars."

"Why?"

They reached his floor.

The doors parted.

In the hallway, he said, "Because I'd already lost everything else."

She grabbed his arm. "Christian, look at me. What are you talking about? What's wrong?"

"My wife. My daughter."

"They left you?"

"They were killed."

"When?"

"Three months ago."

"Three *months* ago? You mean while I was seeing you, you were dealing with this shit? You never even—"

"Not your problem, Letty. Not on my couch. Not here."

"Was it a car wreck?"

"Yeah."

They went on.

"I don't even care about the money," he said, then veered into a wall. He leaned against it. "It was a sign I was looking for."

"What kind of sign?"

"You ever feel like it's all stacked against you, Letty? Like you never had a chance against the house? I just thought that maybe if I bet on black and it hit on black it would mean that things would change. That a corner had been turned. That I didn't have to do what I now have to do."

He grabbed her hands and turned them over.

Exposed her wrists.

Traced a finger down her scars.

Suicide hickeys.

"Must've taken great courage."

"No, not courage. Cowardice. What are you saying?"

"What was your low point, Letty? I can't remember if we ever spoke of it in our sessions."

"Let's get you to your room."

Christian sank down onto the floor.

"Tell me. Please."

"When the court took my son from me. Terminated my parental rights. Night of the ruling . . ." She held up her wrists. "Three bottles of merlot and a straight razor."

"My life is over," he said.

"But it's still yours."

"I don't want it."

She eased down beside him.

"It's like you're in this tunnel," she said. "It's dark, there's no light at the end, and you think it goes on forever." Christian looked up at her, tears returning. "But if you keep putting one foot in front of the other—"

"Even when it's total agony?"

"Especially then. Then one day, you see a speck of light in the distance. And it slowly gets larger. And for the first time, you feel the sensation of moving toward something. Away from all the hurt and the pain and the crushing weight of the past."

"What's it like when you finally emerge?"

"Tell you when I get there."

"You're still in your tunnel?"

"Yeah."

"What keeps you going?"

She could feel herself becoming emotional. Tried to fight it down, but her throat ached with grief.

"I know that when I finally come out into the light that my son will be waiting for me. I want to live to see that version of me."

Christian said, "I have two hundred in cash in my wallet. My room is paid for through tonight. I don't know what happens after that. I don't know where to go. My practice is finished. I don't mean to sound dramatic, but I'm not sure what I'm living for. Why I would continue to breathe in and out."

"For you."

"For me?"

"For the you that one day walks out of that tunnel." Letty stood. "Come on. Let's get you into bed."

"I can't go back to that room and sit there alone in the dark."

Go to meetings. Help others.

"Tell you what," Letty said. "I missed breakfast. Let me take you to lunch. My treat."

"You don't have to do this."

"Actually, I do."

13

Letty changed out of her swimwear and met Christian downstairs.

They walked north toward the tower at the end of the Strip.

It must have been 110 degrees.

Waves of heat glowering off the sidewalks.

The tourists waddling around sweating like disgraced prizefighters.

They took the elevator to the top.

Letty slid the hostess fifty dollars to put them at a window table. Insisted that Christian take the best seat.

Waiting for their waitress to show, he looked like he might nod off right there at the table.

"When's the last time you slept?" Letty asked.

"I don't know. I think I've forgotten how."

"Let me get you some help," she said. "Someone to talk to."

"Psychobabble doesn't work on me. I know all the tricks."

He stared out the window by their table, but she could tell that he didn't see a thing. The restaurant turned imperceptibly. At the moment, their view was west. Miles of glittering sprawl and development. Beyond the city, the desert climbed into a range of spruce-covered mountains.

Letty checked her phone—no missed calls or texts.

"I'm not keeping you, am I?" Christian asked.

"Not at all."

The waitress came.

Letty ordered Christian a coffee.

He reached into his wallet, pulled out two small photos, laid them on the table.

"This is Melanie, my wife. My daughter, Charlie."

Letty lifted the photo of a thirteen- or fourteen-year-old girl. Kneeling in a blue-and-white uniform in front of a goal, holding a soccer ball.

"She's beautiful. And Charlie is short for . . ."

"Charlene."

"That's lovely." Letty reached into her purse, took out a photo of her son—his kindergarten photo.

"Jacob?" Christian asked.

"Yeah, I don't think I ever showed you his picture."

Christian leaned over the table to get a better look.

"Good-looking kid."

Christian collected his photographs and returned them to his wallet with the care and focus of a ritual.

Letty said, "Don't you have family or friends back in Charleston who can help you?"

"They certainly think so."

"But you don't."

"When my girls died, all I got was a bunch of platitudes. Cards that said things like, 'She is just away.' People lining up to tell me they knew what I was going through. I'm never going back."

"Then what will you do?"

"Kill myself. That was the deal I made. I shouldn't be telling you this. I'm a terrible therapist."

"What deal?"

"If I doubled my money, I'd see it as a good omen. I'd try to push on. If I lost, that was it. I was done."

"And there's nothing at this point that might change your mind?"

"Let's be clear. You really don't know me. Don't really know anything about me. You don't love me. You're trying to help me, and, in the sense that I'm not alone in this moment, you are. And it means more to me than I could ever tell you. But don't try to convince me that my life has value. How there's an end to this pain. There isn't. And I know it."

"You told me *my* life had value."

"You shouldn't see me like this," he said. "I don't want it to undo all the progress we made, just because I'm weak."

"You're in this bad spot now. You will feel different one day."

"My girls were my life, and it was over the moment that truck veered into their lane. I'm just trying to pin down my exit strategy."

"How did I miss this?" she asked. "Every week for months, I came to see you. And you were hurting—badly hurting—and I completely missed it. Am I that self-obsessed?"

"No." He smiled. "Let's just say I was that dedicated."

"But you didn't leave town until I did."

"You were my last patient."

"So I was the only thing keeping you from this insanity?"

"No, my loyalty to you as a patient was. This isn't your fault, Letty. You know that, right?"

The food came, but Letty's appetite was shot.

They ate in silence, and when she'd finished her sandwich, she threw her napkin down and fixed her stare on Christian.

He said, "Trying to figure out how to change my mind?"

She shook her head. "It's your call. Your choice. I respect that."

"Thank you."

Letty felt her phone vibrate.

A text from Isaiah: the wynn in 30 . . . we go tonight

Christian must have caught the sudden intensity in her eyes.

He said, "What's wrong?"

"Nothing."

Christian smiled. "So what are *you* doing in Vegas, Letty? I thought you were headed west to see your son."

The waitress brought the check.

Letty waited until she walked away.

"A slight detour. I love Vegas."

"Just here for the shows and the slots, huh?"

She rolled her eyes.

"Let me guess. You're a huge Neil Diamond fan."

Letty said, "How did you know?"

"Wouldn't happen to be running with your old associates? Back to your old tricks? This is a dangerous city for someone with your triggers."

She pulled out enough cash to cover the bill and a twenty-five-percent tip.

Said, "Speaking of, I almost used last night. I did have a drink, but I was on my way to score."

"What happened?"

"Long story short, I went to a meeting instead."

"Good for you. That's great, Letty."

She reached across the table and took hold of his hand.

"Christian, I have to go."

"Thanks for lunch. Thanks for stopping in the lobby when you saw me. You could've walked right on past. I'd never have known."

"This isn't good-bye. You're having dinner with me tonight," she said.

"That means I have to be alive tonight."

She smiled. "Yes, it does."

14

There were now four people waiting inside Letty's room at the Wynn.

Isaiah.

Mark.

And two men she'd never seen before.

Isaiah sprang off the bed, said, "There she is."

As the door closed behind Letty, she noted that the temperature in the room had changed. There was now a palpable pregame energy. The air juiced with nerves, fear, anticipation.

Ize walked over and took her by the arm, said, "Meet Jerrod." She smiled at the tall, rugged man leaning against the dresser. He sported a patchy beard and long walnut-colored hair bundled up into a ponytail.

Isaiah motioned to the other man. "And this is Stu. The three of us helped spread freedom to the Middle East."

"I'm Letty, nice to meet you."

Stu didn't rise from the bed.

Just gave her a slight nod.

His hair was curly and black, and he didn't boast the intimidating build of either Isaiah or Jerrod. But his eyes were as hard as any she'd ever met.

Letty looked at Isaiah. "You intercepted the call?"

He smiled.

"It came in two texts. First the time. Then the room number."

"And it corresponds to a room in this hotel?"

"Tenth floor. East side of the building. In terms of location, it's pretty close to perfect."

"How so?"

"If they took the money any higher, we couldn't rappel out from the room below. We'd have to get a second room closer to ground level. That would mean riding elevators. Exposing ourselves to cameras. It would represent a substantial escalation of risk."

"Rappel?"

"What'd you think, Letty? We were going to tote this shit out in duffel bags through the lobby?"

"What's the time frame?"

"They're moving the money at 0200. To your civilian ass, that's"—he glanced at his watch—"a little more than eleven hours from now." Isaiah looked at Mark. "Our rental van is ready for pickup. Go get it and scope the parking deck one last time."

Letty said, "What about Richter?"

Mark grinned. "One of the cooler things I managed was to program an incoming-call-control feature into Richter's phone."

"English."

"Using the clone, we can call him from any number."

"So tonight," Isaiah said, "just before we suit up, we'll send Richter a text from his Secret Santa, hit him with a fake room number and a fake ETA on Sunday night."

Letty said, "So by the time he realizes the grift . . ."

"We'll all be long gone."

She had to smile. "So what happens now?"

"While Stu and Jerrod bring over the toys, I got a little job for you."

"Okay."

"Your outfit's in the bathroom."

Letty walked down the hallway on the ninth floor.

At the door, she straightened her hunter-green blazer and smoothed her skirt.

Knocked.

A groggy-eyed man answered.

Sleep lines down the right side of his face.

She said, "Mr. Sax?"

"Yes?"

"I'm Amanda, RDM here at the Wynn."

"RDM?"

"Rooms division manager. We've had a maintenance issue crop up. It's impacting the air quality for a segment of rooms on floors eight through eleven. Unfortunately yours is one of them. We're going to need to move you to another room."

"But we're already unpacked and—"

"I understand." She smiled. "Of course, we'll be upgrading you to a Salon Suite, which is nearly two thousand square feet, three times the size of your current room. We'll also be giving you two hundred dollars in chips as a token of our appreciation for your understanding. We're terribly sorry for the inconvenience."

Letty hit a brisk stride on her way back to the Palazzo.

It was almost five o'clock, and she had six hours to kill before Ize's crew was set to rendezvous in the room directly below 1068.

Waiting at the crosswalk on Sands, she dialed Christian's mobile.

"Hi, Letty."

"Something's come up. Can we do an early dinner?"

"Sure, when?"

"I'm free right now," she said. "I just need to change. Let's meet in the lobby in thirty minutes. And wear a coat. I'm taking you someplace special."

"A proper last meal sounds nice."

She asked the concierge to point her toward the best restaurant in town. At first he demurred. A twenty-spot pulled a definitive answer out of him—a French place down the Strip at the MGM Grand. But he feigned doubt that reservations could be procured on such short notice. Forty dollars secured said reservations.

Christian met her at the same bench where she'd found him coming to pieces earlier in the day.

He'd cleaned up. He looked good and smelled good and she told him so, then took his arm as they walked together out into the scorching Vegas evening.

The sun was falling, reflecting off all the chrome and glass.

So hot it seemed like combustion would've been a certainty if there was anything green in sight.

The restaurant sent a limo.

Riding down the boulevard, Letty was struck with the feeling that it wasn't just Christian's last meal, but maybe hers as well. Something about the golden quality of the late light. A sadness, a finality to it.

She stared out the tinted window and thought about her son.

They went all in on a sixteen-course tasting menu.

It was like eating in a library—hushed and reverent—but the food was out of this world. Letty wouldn't drink but insisted Christian have the wine flight. She had been worried going in that the conversation would be heavy, but they found common ground.

Politics.

Children.

Movies.

Letty sat on a velvet couch, propped up with pillows. Rich royal-purple drapes everywhere she looked. Ivy walls. Candlelight.

She had the best lamb she'd ever tasted. Must've been fed gold flakes and the milk of the gods.

The bread cart was legendary.

Like baked clouds.

Everything plated as beautifully as jewelry. The artistic detail more precise than coinage.

Over espressos, Christian said, "I hope that whatever has really brought you to Vegas won't keep you from seeing your son again."

"It's a risk. But I just have this fear that if I were to walk away and drive up to Oregon to be with my son, that within a few months, I'd be broke. Living out of a motel. Strung out. Maybe dead."

"Sounds like your business here could produce the same end result."

"Yeah, but at least I wouldn't be doing it to myself. Truth is, I think about dying all the time. I think about my son finding out. And of all the possible scenarios, Jacob hearing that Mommy was found OD'd and decomposing in a motel is the worst."

"So you are back in the game."

"Are you judging me?"

"No."

"Look, it fills this hole in my soul that I used to throw drugs at."

"Your son doesn't fill it?"

"Only partway."

"So you're saying it's either crime or drugs for you. Can't live without one or the other."

"If I take drugs, I will definitely die. If I . . ."

He finished her sentence: "Steal?"

"Then I'll only maybe die. I'm fighting for my life here, Christian."

"And this thing—it's tonight?"

"Yeah."

"Are you afraid?" he asked.

"Of course."

"And do you find fear to be a help or a hindrance?"

"It helps. For sure."

"How so?"

"It keeps me uncomfortable and sharp. Heightens my senses."

"And you have no doubts about going through with it?"

"Jobs like this—they're the only time I don't think about using. You helped me to see that. You haven't asked for any details," Letty said. "Thank you."

"And you haven't asked me if I'm going through with my plans tonight. Back at you."

"Are you?"

"What exactly *are* you doing?"

They laughed.

"Sounds like a big night for both of us," he said. "The suicide and the thief."

"What would it take?" she asked. "For you to keep on keeping on?"

"It's funny. That's all I've been asking myself lately."

"And?"

"I don't know. Some new experience maybe? Something that made me feel like a different person. Like I was living a different life."

"I hope you find it."

They rode back in the limo.

It was ten o'clock. She could feel the job looming, but she pushed it out of her mind just a little while longer.

She looked up at Christian as they passed Paris Las Vegas. All of the lights and the neon playing across his face like an ecstasy dream.

Then they were parked out front at the Palazzo and the driver was coming around to get their doors.

They embraced in the lobby.

Christian said, "Take care of yourself, Letty."

And she said, "You too. Thanks for everything."

Neither asked the other to reconsider.

Neither said good-bye like how the moment called for it. Like good-bye forever.

The elevator ride up to her room was the only window in which she allowed herself to cry.

15

Room 968 at the Wynn looked like a construction site.

Between the end of the bed and the minibar, a folding ladder stood in a pile of sawdust and plaster dust. A man high up the rungs was waist-deep in the ceiling, a large segment of which lay in pieces on the floor.

Letty locked the door after her and made her way inside.

Detected a muffled hum—the work of a quiet motor.

Dust rained down out of the hole in the ceiling.

She spotted a large black duffel bag in the corner, bulging.

Unzipped it.

Zip ties.

Kevlar vests.

Face masks.

Ball gags.

Shotguns.

"What's this, Ize?" she said, lifting a semiauto tactical shotgun.

"S'all good," he said.

"How exactly is this all good? Aside from the fact that you said 'no guns,' you fire off one shell and you'll wake the entire Strip."

"We won't be firing any shells."

"How's that?"

"Keep digging."

She thrust her hand deeper into the duffel until her fingers grasped a cartridge the size of a twelve-gauge shotgun shell. She lifted out a clear capsule packed with copper wiring and a four-pronged electrode. "TASER XREP" had been engraved into the plastic.

"What is this?" she asked.

"Nasty is what that is. It's a Taser on steroids. Fires out of a shotgun and delivers debilitating pain for up to twenty seconds. I let Jerrod pop me with one. Standard Taser ain't no thing, but I'd hate to meet a man *that* shell can't drop."

"It's not lethal?"

"Nah. Only makes you wish you were dead."

Over by the window, Jerrod was cranking down on a clamp that held a large suction cup to the glass.

Isaiah knelt over an REI store's worth of climbing equipment, just the sight of which tightened Letty's stomach. He was in the process of outfitting each harness with a locking carabiner and an ATC belay device.

She stepped over a neat coil of climbing rope.

Ventured a glance out the window.

The view was east over the lighted pools and a maze of lower roof-tops dotted with AC units. Beyond it all, a golf course shone green in the night.

"It's just seventy feet down to the rooftop below," Isaiah said.

"That's supposed to make me feel better?"

He dropped the harness he'd been working with and rose to his feet.

Tapped the glass.

"Once we get down there, we gotta make it across the convention-center roof. Mark will be waiting for us with the van at the top of the parking deck."

Letty stared at a tower of empty duffel bags in the corner.

"Lot of bags."

"Lot of cash."

"We going to be able to carry it all out?"

"It's a concern—our abundance of riches."

Jerrod said, "Should I start scoring this glass?"

"Yeah, get that shit done." Isaiah lifted one of the duffels. "Assuming the denominations are high, best-case scenario, we fit about four mil into each bag."

Letty watched as Jerrod applied cutting fluid to a wide circle.

Using a Bohle tool kit, he carefully scored a circle with a four-foot diameter into the glass.

"How many pounds we talking?" Letty asked.

"Twenty-two pounds per million dollars."

"That's eighty-eight pounds per bag. I can't carry that."

"Nobody expecting you to. That's all on me and my badass friends. If the haul comes in at thirty-eight or forty, that's ten bags. Three trips across the convention-center rooftop."

"That's a helluva lot of time humping back and forth out in the open."

"Well aware."

"Lot of time for things to fall apart."

"I ever say this would be easy-peasy?"

Jerrod removed the glass cutter, said, "I think I'll go ahead and just take out the circle."

"Might as well."

From a foam-lined aluminum case, Jerrod lifted a new tool.

"What's that?" Letty asked.

"Called a cut opener."

"Cool."

He smiled, eating up the attention. She didn't give a shit, but making nice with Isaiah's cohorts didn't strike her as the worst idea she'd ever had.

He turned a knob. "I'm just setting the tapping force. Watch this."

Holding the device to the surface of the window, he placed the head of the glass tapper to the score line, then squeezed the lever. The cut opened in inch-long segments, slowly forming a perfect circle.

Up in the crawl space, the hum of the motor had stopped.

Stu climbed down out of the ceiling with a circular saw, his face frosted with dust.

Isaiah said, "We happy?"

Stu grinned, wiped a sheen of sweat off his forehead with the sleeve of his shirt.

"I was able to get an angle on the subfloor. Cut out a four-by-four section. Little glitch. There's a slab of marble over top of it. It's gonna take two or three of us to move it. I was only able to lift it a quarter of an inch, and just for a second."

"Well, let's do this. See what we got to work with."

◆

Letty tugged on a pair of latex gloves and went up first.

Richter's contact had said two a.m., but what the hell did that mean? Surely someone would sweep the room before the money showed.

She climbed over a tube of ductwork and emerged into a bathroom.

Swung the beam of her flashlight across the walls.

Swanky.

Giant Jacuzzi tub. Triple vanity. A TV embedded in the mirror. Double-headed shower with more floor space than some apartments she'd rented in her darker days.

She spoke into her headset. "This is not a mirror of our room. It's a large suite. How we doing on time?"

Isaiah hit her back, "No idea, but stay cool. We need some recon."

Letty struggled onto her feet. Her heart banging away.

She moved across the bathroom and through an archway.

Everything dark.

Perfectly quiet.

"Bathroom opens into the master suite."

"Take it slow and low, that is the tempo," Isaiah said. "There could already be cameras or motion sensors in place."

That gave her pause.

"Really?"

"Really."

At the open doorway of the master suite, she killed the light. Stared hard into the darkness.

"Would it be the end of the world if I turned on a proper light?" she asked.

"Nah, go for it."

She found a panel of dimmer switches next to the entertainment center and brought up the lights. Her eyes burned for several seconds.

The living room boasted a wet bar, a desk, an in-room dining area, a high-def plasma screen, and a sitting area adjacent to a floor-to-ceiling window.

The curtains had been swept back.

The desert floor glittering below like crystals in a cave.

Isaiah said, "Are the curtains drawn?"

"No, they're open."

"Close them."

She pulled the curtains, then moved on toward the front door.

Said, "There's a powder room and a room with a massage table by the entrance. Otherwise, we're early to the party."

"All right. We're coming up."

Letty sat on one of the white leather sofas, staring at the time on her iPhone.

12:23 a.m.

One hour and thirty-seven minutes.

Isaiah, Jerrod, and Stu had been circling the suite for the last fifteen, studying the floor plan.

Jerrod said, "We have to already be here when they roll in."

Stu was shaking his head.

They moved out of the bedroom and eased down onto the couches.

"We don't attack until we know what's coming through that door."

Isaiah said, "Intel says six men."

Jerrod said, "What if it's a dozen?"

"Then we go home," Stu said.

"Here's what's going to happen," Isaiah said. "They'll send two men in to sweep the room before they cart in the cash. Confirm all's cool. We can't be in here when that happens. How many cams we got, J?"

"Three, I think. They're with Mark. Where is he, by the way? He was supposed to be here twenty minutes ago."

"We'll put a cam in here, one in the bedroom, one in the bathroom. We let them come in. Let them get comfy. Then we come up through the floor like the fucking Wild Bunch. We're going to be charging in with Taser cartridges. They'll be carrying something with a tad more bite. Full-auto subs if I had to guess. We got no margin for error on this takedown. It has to be fast and quiet. One minute, they sitting around chillin'. The next they're twitching on the floor. We're gonna have to ball gag and zip-tie a minimum of six men inside of twenty seconds."

Isaiah called Mark again but he wasn't answering.

"Something's wrong," he said.

"Yeah," Stu said, "he prolly decided to bail and get stoned. Where'd you find this kid, anyway?"

"He came recommended. Highly."

"Well, he was our uplink to the room. To the hallway. Without him, we got no eyes. Without him . . . I think we're done."

Isaiah bristled. "Done?"

"How we supposed to pull this off coming in blind?"

"You're looking at a ten-million-dollar payday and you talking about walking away that easy?"

"I didn't come out to Vegas to die."

Isaiah looked at Letty.

"What?" she said.

He stood and walked over to the wet bar, opened one of the cabinets. She said, "Hell no."

He smiled. "Not saying it ain't gonna be tight, but I'm thinking we can fit you in there. You gonna be our eyes."

"Hell no."

"Really? That's cool. I'll cram Stu in there and you can bust in here with the big boys, facing down submachine guns with a Taser. I mean, if you feel that'd be your best contribution to the team . . ."

16

It was dark, cramped, and muggy in the cabinet. Letty crouched with her knees drawn tightly to her chest. Her iPhone was set to silent, and she clutched it in her right hand.

1:34 a.m.

With the slab of marble flooring in the bathroom back in place, she couldn't hear the boys in the room below. Nothing, in fact, but the throbbing of her heart like some anxious drum.

What am I doing?

What am I doing?

A week ago a waitress.

Now this?

Robbing a casino?

But it was beyond exhilarating, and she hadn't even thought of using in hours.

Her phone lit up—Isaiah texting.

call if you can

She dialed.

"Tell me you found Mark."

"He's AWOL."

"Seriously?"

"Still ain't answering."

"Shit."

"He was our ride out of Dodge. Had the radio, the scanners down cold."

"So what now?"

"What now? Nothing now. We stand the fuck down." She felt a flare of relief, a pang of regret. "I hate this," he said, "but we gotta be ready to roll. Can't just camp out on the roof of the convention center with nine duffel bags full of cash. Hoping to somehow figure this shit out before the sun rises and the SWAT rolls in."

Letty closed her eyes, surprised as the needle swung firmly into regret.

"It's the score of a lifetime," she said.

"You think *I* need to hear that shit?"

"I have an idea," she said.

"What?"

"We need a driver, right? That's all?"

"Yeah."

"Call you back."

In the darkness of the cabinet, she searched her call history.

Please don't have done anything stupid. Please. Please. Please.

Christian answered, "Hello?"

"Hey, it's Letty. I wake you?"

"No."

"You okay?"

"I haven't done anything yet, if that's what you're calling about."

"I have something to ask you."

"Thought you weren't going to try and save me."

"I'm not." *Not entirely true.* She cracked the cabinet door so she could keep an eye on the entrance to the suite.

"What's going on, Letty?"

"Remember when I asked you what it would take for you to want to live?"

"Yeah."

"And you said a new experience."

"Right."

"What if I could give you that? Right now."

"You could give me a new experience."

"Yes."

"I wasn't talking about sex, Letty. Much as I like you—"

"I'm not either."

"So what are you talking about?"

"What kind of car did you drive out to Vegas?"

"Excuse me?"

"What kind of car did you drive here?"

"A Suburban. Why?"

She felt her heart swell with hope, said, "You really want a taste of something new? Something so far out of your realm of experience, it's gonna blow your mind?"

"Yes, Letty."

"Even if it's dangerous?"

"Especially."

"Fast as you can, bring your Suburban over to the Wynn. I'm going to give you the phone number of a man named Isaiah. He'll tell you exactly what to do."

"What is this, Letty?"

Sure about this?

All in.

"We're robbing the casino in less than one hour. Our driver is MIA. This is your chance to step in, take his place, and earn over a million dollars for a night's work."

The silence on the other end of the line went on and on.

She could just hear the sound of the television bleeding through. Some violent TV show or film. A man screaming through a gag.

She said, "Christian? You there?"

"Is this for real?"

"I swear to you. Look, I hate to pressure you, but our backs are against the wall. You ever see the movie *Heat*?"

"Sure. It's in my top ten."

"Remember when De Niro goes to the diner and hires the black guy from the Allstate commercials to be his driver?"

"Yeah."

"Remember how it's a right-then-and-there, in-or-out, yes-or-no proposition?"

"I do."

"Well, this is exactly like that. I need a yes or no right now. And before you answer, I have to be straight with you. This is beyond dangerous. If it all comes off the rails, you could be killed. If we're caught, you could go to prison for a long time."

More silence.

She said, "Did I just totally call your bluff, or what?"

"You called it. Damn. You called it. But you know what?"

"What?"

"It wasn't a bluff."

❖

"No way."

"Isaiah—"

"No way. He's a civilian."

"So what? He knows how to drive, doesn't he? We aren't asking him to do hostage control."

"And you've known him *how* long?"

"I met him when I lived in Charleston. Six months."

"You gotta be kidding me. What's he doing in Vegas?"

"He lost his family recently. He's suicidal. Nothing to live for."

"These are selling points?"

"You want this money or not, Isaiah? How many shots come along in your lifetime to make a score like this?" Finally, a pause. She could almost hear the gears turning. Said, "It's 1:44, Isaiah. Someone's coming through that door any minute now, and you know it."

"Bringing somebody in I never worked with, never heard of, this late in the game, this big of a job. No scanners, no radio. We'll be blind."

"What other options do we have? It's this or walk away right now."

"You right. You right."

"So you want to walk away? Pack up all your toys and go home?"

Silence.

She said, "Am I sitting tight or coming back down?"

At 1:57 a.m., she heard the electronic chiming of the door's locking mechanism.

Her legs had gone numb ten minutes ago, a pins-and-needles sensation sparkling from her hips down to her toes.

The discomfort vanished.

The lights flicked on.

Letty cracked the cabinet door open just a sliver.

A suited man with a shaved head and neatly trimmed goatee had entered. He was built like a vending machine. Carried a MAC-10 with a long magazine and suppressor, the machine pistol dangling from a shoulder strap.

He glanced into the powder room, the massage room.

Walked past the dining table, then turned, moving toward Letty's cabinet.

She let her door close fully.

Listening as his wingtips sank into the plush carpet, his wool pants swishing.

She caught a whiff of overbearing cologne.

Finally dared to breathe again when his footsteps trailed off toward the bedroom. She lifted her phone, banged out a text to Isaiah as the man's footfalls echoed off the marble in the bathroom.

```
1 man just entered
doing walk through
```

Isaiah responded in her headset. "Copy that. Just be cool."

The man emerged from the bedroom and walked into the living room. He lifted the shoulder strap over his head and set the machine pistol on the glass-topped coffee table. Tugged a small radio from an inner pocket in his jacket, said, "Clear."

Thirty seconds later, that electronic chiming repeated.

There was enough noise as the men entered for Letty to whisper into her microphone.

"Ize, can you hear me?"

"Loud and clear."

She whispered, "Three, make that four men have just entered."

"In addition to the first guy?"

"Yeah. Five total. All armed. Shotguns. Machine guns. Pistols. And still more are coming. A whole line of them."

"All muscle?"

"No, they're pushing carts."

"What's on the carts?"

"Cages. Covered in wire mesh."

"Our money?"

She liked the sound of that.

Said, "Oh my God."

"What?"

"I've just never seen so much. That makes six. Six carts they rolled in here."

"Is it our money?"

"Oh yeah. And there's a shit-ton of it. Two more guards have entered."

"Seven total?"

"You guys can handle seven, right?"

The cart pushers departed, leaving the half dozen carts grouped near the dining area.

The front door closed.

A man armed with a subcompact Glock took a post by the entrance.

The other six retired to sofas in the living room.

One of them spoke into a radio. "We're in, locked down, all secure."

Letty whispered, "They're getting settled. One man is standing by the door, the other six are in the living area. Wait."

One of the men stood. He moved over to the carts and, on top of one of them, placed a small device mounted to a tripod. It began to revolve slowly.

"What's happening?" Isaiah asked.

"Not sure yet. Stand by."

The man pressed a button on the device, said into his radio, "Visual installed. Confirm."

As he returned to the sofa, Letty said, "They set up a camera. It turns, takes in the entire room."

"It's okay. We planned for this contingency."

"So what happens now?"

"Sit tight."

The radio silence unnerved her. The pain in her legs was back with a vengeance. Through the crack between the door and the cabinet, she watched the guards.

Everyone black-suited. None younger than thirty, none older than forty-five.

Each exuding his own special brand of ex-military, fucked-by-life hardness.

Two of the men chatted about an upcoming fight at Caesars.

One just stared.

Another took laps around the room.

She startled when Isaiah came through her earpiece.

He said, "Report."

"One guard is still by the door. Five seated in the living area. One on his feet near the TV."

"Have they been making regular trips into the bedroom or bathroom?"

"Just once."

"Are the curtains still drawn?"

"Yes."

"Perfect. How *you* feeling?"

"Scared."

"It's showtime."

"Even with the camera rolling?"

"Yes. When I say go, I want you to climb out of the cabinet. Let them see you. Distract them. Engage them. Just don't get yourself shot."

"How much time do you need?"

"Ten, maybe fifteen seconds."

Her heart rate tripled.

She began to perspire.

Heard Isaiah say, "Stu? Jerrod? Ten seconds." And then, "Letisha?"

"Yes."

"You got your head on straight for this?"

"Absolutely."

"Because the next hour is going to take a few years off your life."

"I'll bill you for the Botox."

There was a four-second pause, and then Isaiah said, "Go."

17

Letty tugged down her Barbie Halloween mask.

Her iPhone lit up with a text as she reached for the door.

Christian: `never in my life felt so alive thank you`

She nudged the door open and crawled out of the cabinet onto the carpet.

No one saw her.

She slipped out of sight behind the bar, made herself take three deep breaths, flooding her lungs with oxygen.

She tried to stand but her legs were still numb. Frantically, she squeezed her calves. The tingling burn of sensation roared back.

Up onto her feet.

Got her elbows on the granite bar.

For what seemed like ages, nothing happened.

She couldn't see the guard by the entrance, but the six men in the living room carried on just as before.

She opened her mouth.

The words fell out.

"What a sausage fest. Could I get any of you gentlemen a drink?"

The air went out of the room.

Six heads turning.

The seventh guard stepping out from the entranceway with an expression of pure disbelief spreading across his face.

Three men were already on their feet, reaching for weapons, the others rising.

Someone said, "How the hell—"

Letty said, "I sort of come with the room."

The tallest, oldest of the bunch stepped forward and trained his Glock on the center of her chest.

Thank God—he was blocking the camera from seeing her.

He said, "How did you get into this room?"

"Did you not just hear me?"

"You have no idea the world of shit you have just brought down on yourself."

Letty smiled through the mask, making sure to keep her hands visible and still.

"Worlds of shit are all I know, dude."

She couldn't be sure, but she thought she heard the faintest sound coming through the wall—something sliding across the bathroom floor.

In her ear, Isaiah whispered through a strained voice, "Keep him talking, we're almost in."

She said, "Are you sure you don't want that drink? Gotta be honest. You all seem a little tense."

The man glanced at the wide-load who had been on the door.

"You were first in, asshole. Where'd she come from?"

"I checked everywhere."

"Really." He came another step forward, Letty growing increasingly uneasy with that black hole of death staring her down. Wasn't the first time, but you never got used to it. The difference between you being here and not—just the smallest movement of a finger.

Isaiah said, "Letty, get down."

She dropped.

By the time she hit the carpet, the lights had gone out.

Instinct drove her to cover her head with her arms.

She heard confused shouting.

Footfalls on carpet.

Bursts of suppressed submachine-gun fire, rounds chewing through the drywall.

Then the sound of snapping filled the room, interspersed with the *shuck-shuck* of shotguns pumping, more snapping, men screaming.

Isaiah's voice: "Go, go, go."

Jerrod: "Hit him again."

Men groaning, struggling against the electrical current.

Stu said, "Lights back in ten. Disable the camera."

Jerrod: "It's toast."

Letty sat up, grabbed hold of the edge of the bar, and hauled herself back onto her feet.

Isaiah said, "Everyone secure?"

"Yep."

"Yes."

Stu said, "Five seconds. Remove goggles."

"Done."

"Done."

"Three, two, one."

The lights returned.

What a difference thirty seconds had made.

Letty said, "Color me impressed."

Six of the seven guards lay on their stomachs, hog-tied with zip ties, twitching with the remnants of Taser shock. The barbed electrodes were still embedded in their chests, the propulsion cartridges dangling by wires.

Stu and Jerrod straddled two of the men, tightening ball gags around the backs of their heads. Isaiah sat on the chest of the seventh, who wasn't gagged. Ize held a radio in one hand, a Fairbairn-Sykes in the other, the knifepoint digging under the man's right eye.

Letty's crew looked more like mercs than thieves. Outfitted in close-fitting night camo. Night-vision goggles hanging from their necks. Super 90s strapped to their backs. All wearing neoprene face masks screen printed with demonic-looking clown faces.

Isaiah said to the guard pinned under his weight, "Tell them the camera shorted out, and to send someone up with a spare. I double-dog dare you to try a goddamn thing."

The man nodded.

Isaiah clicked "Talk."

"Hey, it's Matt, over."

"Copy, we lost visual, over."

Letty walked out from behind the bar into the living room.

"Yeah, the camera crapped out. Send up a new one."

"Copy that. En route."

Isaiah set the radio down on the carpet. "Very good. Very good, Matt."

"You'll never make it out," Matt said. "Not in a million years."

"Well, if it was easy, any old goon could do it. Maybe even you."

Stu had moved over to the cages.

"What do you see, my man?" Isaiah asked.

"Four-jaw independent chuck, top-reversible D-4 cam lock."

"Same on each cage?"

"Yep."

"This happy news or bad news?"

Stu said, "It's just news. Nothing I didn't plan for." He reached into his pocket and tossed Isaiah a chunk of gray metal the size of a chalkboard eraser.

"Stick that magnet under the doorknob."

Stu hurried off toward the bedroom.

Jerrod followed.

The guards lay still on the floor all around them, just panting now. With the red ball gags in their mouths, they reminded Letty of roasting pigs. She glanced back at the wall behind the bar. A spray pattern—two dozen holes—arced up toward the ceiling.

Isaiah gagged his man and stood.

He headed to the entrance, glanced through the peephole.

Stu and Jerrod returned, Jerrod toting the empty duffel bags under one arm, Stu carrying a small, beefy drill.

He hit the first cage, had the lock drilled out and off in less than forty-five seconds.

Jerrod glanced at Letty, said, "Shall we?"

He pulled open the door to the first cage. Letty reached in. Both hands grabbing crisp stacks of hundreds bound with black wrappers. On each wrapper, "10,000" had been printed in gold. The cube of money was twenty stacks high, twenty-five packets per story.

$5 million per cart.

Six carts.

$30 million.

Give or take.

Something so satisfying about dropping them into the duffel, the smell of ink and paper filling the room.

Letty could feel the eyes of the guards on her as she worked. Stu was already through the third lock, and she and Jerrod had nearly filled the second duffel.

"Report," Isaiah called from the door.

"Cruising, brother," Stu said. "What's our time in?"

"Two minutes, fifty-five seconds."

Jerrod zipped the first two duffels, pushed them aside.

They started in on the third cage.

Aside from the whine of the drill, they worked with a quiet intensity. The minutes whirred past with a staggering paradox of speed and timelessness.

So much adrenaline raging through Letty's system it felt like they'd been in this room for hours.

Stu drilled out the last lock. Then he lifted something that resembled a TSA wand and started moving it slowly over the duffel bags.

"We got company," Isaiah said. "One guy."

"Need an assist?" Jerrod asked.

"What are you implying, brother?"

"Armed?"

"Just stay on task. I got this."

There was a knock at the door.

Letty looked up. Would've missed the entire thing if she'd blinked.

Isaiah opened the door, dragged a good-looking Latino into the suite, and turned his lights out with an elbow strike.

Ten seconds later, the man was bound and gagged with the rest of them.

Isaiah jogged over as Stu was wanding the last cage.

"We happy?"

"Yeah, none of the cash is chipped."

"What does that mean?" Letty asked.

"It means they can't track it."

Letty packed the last armful of stacks into a duffel and zipped it up. Isaiah, Stu, and Jerrod had already carried most of the bags into the bathroom. Letty tried to lift one, but it didn't weigh much less than she did. It was all she could do to drag it across the carpet.

Halfway to the bedroom, she heard the guard's radio.

A man's voice. Deep, raspy.

"Matt, did your camera show up? Over."

Letty dropped the duffel, rushed back. She turned Matt over, unfastened his ball gag, and grabbed the radio. The closest weapon was a MAC-10 lying on the coffee table.

She grabbed it, held it under the man's chin.

"Matt, do you copy? Over."

She said, "Tell him he just showed up and that you'll be back online momentarily. Say just those exact words."

"Letty, what's up?" Isaiah from the bedroom.

She held up her finger.

Stared straight into Matt's eyes, saw plenty of steel there, but some fear, too.

Hopefully enough.

As she held the radio to his mouth, it suddenly occurred to her what she was doing. That she was threatening a man with his life. Of course she wouldn't pull the trigger if he sold them out, but still—a line had appeared and she'd crossed it.

Without hesitation.

Pure reaction.

Her first armed robbery.

You have no choice. You have to get out of this hotel right now.

Matt spoke into the radio, "He just showed up. We're installing it now. Be back online momentarily. Over."

"Copy that."

She took the radio and bolted back into the bedroom.

The duffels were gone and Jerrod was just lowering himself down through the crawl space.

She stopped at the edge of the gaping hole and got down onto her knees. Isaiah gave her a hand over the lip of the marble. She found her footing in the crawl space, the urge to be out of this mess, out of this hotel, this city, overpowering.

A sense of panic, of time running out, enveloping her.

Then she was climbing down the ladder into room 968, listening to the marble slab slide back into place. The soles of Isaiah's tactical boots descended toward her as he maneuvered through the ductwork.

18

It took Letty four tries to get her left leg through the harness.

Isaiah watching her from the window.

He said, "You gotta lock that shit down."

"Lock what down?"

"Your panic."

Stu had rappelled out the window four minutes ago. Jerrod right on his heels. Now Ize had the last three duffel bags on belay, smoothly lowering two hundred and fifty pounds of cash—$12 million—to the convention-center roof.

The radio crackled again.

A rod of tension shot through Letty's entire body.

Isaiah unclipped his locking carabiner from his harness and moved over to the bed.

"Matt, we still have no visual, over."

Isaiah lifted the radio, pulled off a passable impersonation.

"This one doesn't work either, over."

"Are you messing with me? Over."

"Nope. Over."

"I'm bringing one up personally. Over."

"Copy that."

"See you in five."

Isaiah said, "Now you can panic." He grabbed her harness, gave it a hard tug. "Ever rappelled before?"

"No." She could feel a wave of nausea coming on.

"Easiest thing in the world."

"I'm sure."

As they approached the gaping hole in the window, Letty felt the night heat of Vegas and the smell of the Strip and the desert ripping through. Sage and car and restaurant exhaust.

Isaiah had rigged a sophisticated anchor system of webbing to the bed frame.

"I don't want to die," Letty said.

A black rope had been halved and thrown out the window.

"Go ahead, look," Isaiah said. "You need to see where you're going."

She edged up to the glass, poked her head through.

"Oh Jesus Christ."

Stomach swirling. Body in full revolt against this.

Stu and Jerrod the size of Lego men far below.

The curve of the building a dizzying mindfuck.

"We should've gone over this before," Letty said.

Isaiah grabbed her belay device, threaded the rope through, then locked everything into the carabiner on her harness.

"I'm scared," she said.

"I hear that. But personally . . . I'd rather fall and die than be in this room when hotel security busts through. You feel me?"

She nodded.

He grabbed her hands, put her left on the rope near the belay device, her right on the rope farther back.

"This belay device is your friend, your brake. When the rope is back here"—he touched her right hand to her hip—"you won't move. When you raise it up, it'll allow the rope to feed through. You'll drop."

Her heart was going like mad.

"Do not let your left hand get too close to the belay device. It'll chew it up. You'll let go and die."

The radio crackled. "On my way, Matt. Say, did you ever send Mario down? He never showed, isn't responding, over."

Isaiah said, "Look in my eyes." She did. "You go down in a sitting position. Control your speed."

"I can't do this."

"You have to do this." He helped her up onto the lip of the glass.

"I can't," she said.

"You been through worse than this. Put your right hand in the brake position." She clutched it, held it to her hip. "You ain't gotta squeeze so hard. Relax. Now lean back."

"I can't."

"Stop saying that."

"Matt, do you copy? Over."

"Lean. Back."

She hung her ass out over the gaping darkness, her stomach turning itself inside out.

"Now raise your right hand slowly, until you feel the rope begin to glide through the belay device."

"I—"

"Do it!"

"Matt, do you copy? Over."

She raised the rope off her hip.

Isaiah smiled at her from inside the room, said, "There you go, now let it slide through your grasp, but not too fast."

She opened her fingers, felt the rope move through.

She dropped a foot.

"Keep it going," Isaiah said, "and I hate to rush you, but I do need you to hurry the fuck up."

She descended in erratic bursts.

The sensation of plummeting to her death never out of her mind.

Twenty feet below their window, she lowered past a room where the curtains had not been drawn. Glimpsed a couple watching television in bed less than ten feet away, their faces awash in high-def glow.

She ventured a glimpse down, surprised to see that she was already halfway to the ground. Lifting her right hand as far off her hip as she'd yet dared, she felt the rope streaming through her loosened grasp. The balls of her feet bounced off the windows. For a fraction of a second, it was almost fun.

She touched solid ground, her legs buckling, relief blazing through her veins.

Jerrod caught her before she fell.

They stood at the edge of a field of commercial AC units that were noisy as turboprops. He unscrewed her locking carabiner, ripped the rest of the rope through her belay device, and said, "She's down, Ize. Let's blow."

Letty looked around—too dark to see much of anything beyond the fact that Stu and all but two of the bags were gone.

She was about to ask where he was when Isaiah hit the ground beside her.

She said, "Wow, you've done that a few times."

"Once or twice."

The men shouldered the last two duffels.

Jerrod led the way, threading between the roaring AC vents.

"How much time do we have?" Letty asked as they ran.

"They know something's up. But we magnetized the lock in the suite. No keycard will get them through. Yelling for someone to let them in won't get them through. They'll have to break it down."

"And then?"

She was having to shout to be heard.

"I don't know," he said. "The guards saw us go through the bedroom and disappear. I moved the marble quietly, but I'm guessing they'll connect the dots in a hurry. Or else someone will spot us on this rooftop."

"Cameras up here?"

"Possibly. Whether or not they catch us at this point will depend on how quickly they can lock down all exits from the property. And if they've conceived of a theft like this."

They climbed over a four-foot wall.

Jerrod said, "Almost there."

Letty spotted the shadow of Stu up ahead.

They reached him.

Isaiah and Jerrod let the bags slough off their shoulders. She peered over the ledge. The wall dropped six feet to the top level of a parking deck. A white Suburban idled below, the rear cargo doors thrown open.

The parking deck was well lit, inhabited by a smattering of vehicles, but otherwise still and quiet.

"Your boy showed," Isaiah said. He looked at Jerrod and Stu, said, "Homestretch. There will be cameras. Move like the wind, gentlemen."

He hoisted a bag, swung it over the ledge, let it fall to the concrete on the other side.

The remaining bags followed.

Then the men.

Then Letty, climbing over last, letting her feet hang for a beat before dropping.

The Suburban's rear seating had been removed.

Stu loaded the final duffel as Letty hurried around the back and climbed up into the front passenger seat.

She pulled off her mask and smiled at Christian.

"Good to see you again," he said.

Ize and his crew piled in, doors slamming.

Isaiah said, "Christian, glad you could make it."

Christian shifted into gear. "Where to?"

"95 North."

Christian drove down the ramp into the parking garage.

A tense silence descending over the car.

After the second overly hard turn, Isaiah said, "Just drive cool, my man. This ain't the movies. No one's chasing us yet."

Letty checked her iPhone—2:23.

Hard to believe that only twenty-three minutes had elapsed since the guards had walked into that suite. She'd worried enough in that time span for three lifetimes.

Each corner Christian turned ratcheted the knot in her stomach a little tighter.

Her hands trembled. She tried to steady them, but she was too amped.

She looked over, studied Christian. "You all right?" she asked.

He nodded, but he looked scared as hell.

The road out of the garage seemed to go on forever, like the Penrose stairs.

Turn.

After turn.

After turn.

Letty stared out the window, watching all the paint jobs of the cars gleaming under the harsh light.

Something reached her through the glass. She lowered her window two inches.

There it was—the screech of tires across smooth concrete.

She said, "Someone's coming up fast."

Jerrod said, "Ize? Should he pull into an open space? Let them pass?"

"Hell no. All likelihood, they got a vehicle description. We need to get the fuck out. Just drive, my man. And try not to crash."

The screeching drew closer.

Letty heard Isaiah's glass hum down, turned just in time to see him climbing up onto his knees, pointing an AR-15 through his window.

She buckled her seat belt.

Christian took a hard, squealing turn.

A black Escalade ripped into view.

Isaiah opened up.

Three bursts on full auto, a smear of silver-rimmed holes starring the engine and driver-side door of the Escalade. Its right front tire blew. Christian gunned the Suburban, its back end jutting left, smashing into the side of the Escalade as it passed.

"Down!" Isaiah screamed.

The back window of the Suburban exploded in a splash of safety glass, bullets chinking into the cargo doors.

Christian cranked it around one last curve.

Letty saw it first—a black strip lying across the exit lane up ahead.

"Spikes!" she yelled. "Other lane!"

Christian steered over a six-inch concrete median with a violent shudder that seemed to tear apart the undercarriage. The entrance gate snapped off as they punched through and made a hard, blind turn into traffic.

They accelerated down Las Vegas Boulevard.

The Strip still rocking at two thirty in the morning.

"Nicely done," Isaiah said. "Now hang a left at the next intersection."

Letty glanced back. Traffic moved slowly but there was plenty of it.

The curve of the Wynn fell away.

She heard frantic honking, accompanied by a symphony of sirens. Several SUVs a few hundred yards back were fighting their way through traffic with little success.

"Radio and scanner would be nice," Stu said.

"Doing the best we can, brother."

Letty said, "They'll put out a description of the Suburban, right?"

"APB, no doubt."

They lucked out, caught a protected green arrow at the next intersection.

Christian turned onto Desert Inn Road.

Compared to the Strip, this street was practically vacant.

Christian said, "Should I speed or just—"

"Hell yes, speed. We just knocked over a casino, son."

The man pushed the gas pedal into the floor.

They screamed past a vacant lot where a new hotel was in its foundational infancy.

Then Trump Tower.

"Let's get off the beaten path," Isaiah said.

"Any particular direction?"

"Just keep us moving north."

They drove residential streets, dead quiet at this hour.

Isaiah said, "Now you keep it under control. Only drive like a maniac if you see the po-po coming."

Letty leaned against the glass. Tried to steady her rampant pulse, but it wouldn't slow. They hadn't just robbed at gunpoint. She'd been part of a crew that had fired on casino security. Isaiah could have killed the driver. And if the cops showed, tried to take them down, was there any doubt that a gunfight of epic proportions would ensue?

How did you let it get this far?

Because I needed it to.

Are you really this person, Letisha Dobesh?

She smiled.

Because she was.

Because she loved it.

19

On the edge of town, Isaiah directed Christian into the boondocks of a Walmart Supercenter parking lot. It was surprisingly busy considering the hour. This far out from the epicenter of Save-Money-Live-Better Land was the territory of Winnebagos, car campers, and one U-Haul. Specifically, a 4 × 8 trailer already rigged to the towing package of a car that had piqued Letty's fear several days ago in Arizona.

Isaiah's black Tundra.

Letty climbed out and raised the door.

The four men had the trailer loaded inside of thirty seconds.

They hit US 95 at three a.m.

Blasted north.

Isaiah driving.

By three fifteen, the suburban sprawl had begun to relent.

Patches of lightless, unsettled desert scrolling past with greater frequency.

The glow of the Strip dwindled in the rearview mirror.

The sky trading the absurdity of the Vegas skyline for honest-to-God stars.

Even forty miles out of town, no one spoke.

As if their success up to this moment hinged upon a collective silence.

By four o'clock in the morning they were tearing through a landscape that looked ready-made for missile testing.

Scorched earth.

Joyless mountains.

No trees.

Snakeskin country.

It was Isaiah who finally broke the silence.

Said, "Christian. I'd roll with you again. You are absolutely badass."

Letty looked back, saw Christian smirking.

"And you, Letty," Isaiah said. She could hear the celebration beginning to build in his voice. "Wasn't for you, we wouldn't be here."

She said, "I told Christian he'd make at least a million."

"Nope," Isaiah said. "My man stepped up on a moment's notice. Saved the day. Let's call it one point five. How you guys know each other back wherever you from?"

"He's my therapist."

"No, seriously."

They rode toward Death Valley under a star-blown sky.

Letty's adrenaline charge had tapped out.

She hadn't been this dog-tired since the birth of her son.

Ize turned off the highway.

For several miles, they bumped along a one-lane road that snaked through the creosote.

The stars had just begun to fade and the sky to draw color when Letty spotted structures in the distance.

The road curved toward a collection of buildings. At first, she mistook them for a town, but on approach, she saw they were nothing but skeletons. Broken framework profiled against the sky.

Isaiah eased to a stop in front of the remnants of a three-story building.

The only part still standing was its facade.

The rest had been reduced to crumbling mortar.

Ize killed the ignition.

The silence that flooded in was graveyard quiet.

Through the dusty windshield, Letty spotted four cars parked a little ways down the road.

"Whose are those?" she asked.

"Ours," Isaiah said. "They're just rentals. I figured we'd split the dough here. Go our separate ways."

Christian was sitting in the back between Stu and Jerrod.

He cleared his throat, said, "You're absolutely sure we're safe here?"

Isaiah glanced back between the front seats.

"US 95 South. US 93 South. I-15 South. I-15 North. US 93 North. US 95 North. Six main arteries out of Vegas. They're looking for a vehicle that matches your white Suburban. They will check every motel and hotel within three or four hours, which is why we aren't taking that chance. Why don't you let the professionals do the thinking, my man. You're in good hands."

They climbed out.

It was almost cold in the desert ghost town.

No wind.

Letty glanced back the way they'd come. The dust trail of their passage beginning to settle.

Everywhere she looked—emptiness.

Isaiah walked out into the middle of the road. He stared off at the distant hills.

Then laughed—long and low.

Jerrod and Stu moved toward him, and as he turned, the trio embraced.

A fierce, sudden, emotional huddle.

"I'm so proud. We did it, boys. We did it. They're gonna make movies about us."

"Yeah," Christian said. "And with a big surprise ending."

Letty looked across the hood of Ize's Tundra.

It took her a second to process Christian standing in the road with an AR-15 pulled snug against his shoulder, sighting down the Marines.

"Gentlemen," he said. "Raise your hands and get down on your knees."

Isaiah's head tilted. "What the fuck—"

The gunshot exploded across the desert, the round punching through the windshield of one of the rentals.

"Next shot goes through your eye. *Ize.*"

Isaiah, Stu, and Jerrod exchanged glances.

They slowly lifted their arms, got down on their knees.

"Join them, Letty."

"What are you doing, Christian?"

"You're going to make me kill somebody, aren't you?"

She moved around the front of the car.

"Christian," Isaiah said. "You want more money? An even split? We can do that. This hard-bargaining shit ain't necessary. We're reasonable men."

Letty eased down into the dirt.

"Your offer of one point five million was generous, but I think I'll have to settle for everything. Where are the keys to the Tundra, Isaiah?"

"Ignition."

"Where are the keys to the rentals?"

"Center console."

Christian fired eight shots in rapid succession.

Letty heard the air hissing out of the tires of the cars behind them.

"Everyone, flat on your stomach, spread out your hands."

"I'll find you," Isaiah said.

Christian backed away, keeping the gun on them as he approached the driver-side door of the Tundra.

"I could kill you all right here, leave you in the desert. Perhaps you should be thanking me for allowing you to live instead of making empty threats."

"Nothing empty about them, my man."

"Christian, please," Letty said.

"Thank me, Ize," Christian said.

"Fuck you."

"Thank me or you die right now."

"Thank you," Isaiah said through gritted teeth.

"You're welcome."

Letty watched as Christian opened the door.

Isaiah said under his breath, "Anybody packing?"

"No."

"No."

Jerrod said, "I can get there. I can stop this."

"He can shoot," Isaiah said. "In case you missed the part where he went eight for eight on those tires."

Christian reached into the car.

He cranked the engine.

Isaiah said, "I ain't believing this shit."

Christian jumped in, slammed the door, the engine revving.

The Tundra lurched toward them.

Letty didn't even have time to get to her feet.

Just rolled out of the way as the tires slung rocks and dirt, the rubber tread passing inches from her head.

She sat up, coughing, wiping dust out of her eyes.

Isaiah's Tundra sped off down the dirt road, taillights shrinking into the dawn.

Isaiah jumped to his feet, sprinted twenty yards.

He planted his feet and screamed at the sky, his voice racing across the wasted landscape, ricocheting between the buildings in the ghost town.

He turned and started back toward the group, toward Letty.

When he was ten feet away, she noticed the knife in his hand.

"Isaiah, please."

She scrambled onto her feet, backpedaling.

"You," he said. "You did this."

"I don't know what you're talking about."

"You brought Christian in."

"I had no idea."

He rushed her, swept her off her feet.

She struck the ground hard enough to drive the air out of her lungs.

Isaiah—all 220 pounds of him—perched on her chest, his knees pinning her arms to the hardpan.

He dug the knifepoint into her face.

"I ought to carve you up right here. Leave you for the buzzards."

"I didn't—"

"Where did you find him?"

"I told you. He was my therapist. I ran into him at the Palazzo. He was suicidal. Had lost his family several months ago. He told me he'd come to Vegas to kill himself."

Isaiah leaned in close.

"What else do you know about him?"

"Nothing. I only saw him in sessions."

"You think he shoots like a shrink? Think he drives getaway like a shrink?"

"I'm more stunned than you are, Ize. I swear to you. I told that man my darkest secrets for six months."

"Something ain't right here." He drew the blade softly across her throat. "I'll find him," Isaiah said. "And when I do, me and Christian will have a talk. He will tell me all of his secrets. If I find out—"

"You won't, because I didn't. If you want to kill me because I got played, go for it. But I'd never sell my partners down the river."

Isaiah pushed the blade against her carotid.

Stu and Jerrod had wandered over. They stood behind Isaiah, staring down at her.

"What do you think, boys?" he asked. "Feel like watching her bleed?"

20

Letty walked alone down the dirt road away from the ghost town, back toward the highway.

Isaiah, Stu, and Jerrod had gone ahead.

She couldn't see them anymore.

The sun crested a range of barren hills.

The desert went supernova.

She walked on, shoes scraping dirt.

Buzzards circled.

With each step, she became more thirsty, more exhausted, more humiliated.

Occasionally, blinding silver specks would streak across the far horizon. It was the highway, still miles away.

The sun was high by the time she reached the pavement, beating down with a kind of angry purpose.

There was no sign of Isaiah and the boys.

Sweat poured out of her.

She walked twenty feet down the road and then her legs failed.

She dropped.

Sat down in the dirt.

Stunned, crushed, confused, enraged.

Still trying to process what had happened.

If she wasn't mistaken, it was four or five miles back to Beatty, the last town they'd passed through. But she was in no condition to make the trek. She'd left her purse and iPhone in Ize's Tundra. Had a twenty-dollar bill shoved down one of her socks, but not another penny, credit card, or form of identification to her name.

There was nothing coming in either direction.

The heat wafting off the blacktop like a furnace.

Scorpions watching her from the shade.

She couched her face between her knees and shut her eyes.

The sound of an approaching car brought her head up.

For a moment, she didn't know where she was.

She hoisted her arm into the air and raised her thumb.

A Prius screamed past, kept going.

The sun bore down from directly overhead, and she could feel herself beginning to come apart.

You have to get up.

You have to walk to town.

You cannot just sit here and wait for a Good Samaritan to stop.

Because they don't exist anymore.

She walked up the shoulder of the highway, swatting at the swarm of flies and gnats that had been attracted by her salt-tinged sweat.

In the distance, the mini-roar of an engine.

She looked up.

Couldn't see anything through the brutal glare.

Just blinding chrome and glass.

Thinking, *If I took my top off, would they stop?*

Could you handle that rejection if they didn't?

She raised her arm, held out her thumb, but didn't slow her pace.

Kept walking as she shielded her eyes.

The car streaked past.

She traded her thumb for a middle finger.

But something was different with this one.

The pitch of its engine had dropped.

She stopped, made a slow, staggering turn.

Damn.

Somebody had actually pulled over.

She stumbled toward the vehicle, moving as fast as she could manage, some part of her fearing that as she drew near it would turn into a mirage.

But the image held.

A burgundy Chevy Astro with deeply tinted windows.

She sidled up to the van's front passenger door, yanked it open, climbed up into the seat. The air-conditioning was crisp and roaring out of the vents.

She looked over at the driver, her head spinning, unwieldy.

Said, "I can't thank you e—"

At first, she thought she was hallucinating.

A symptom of heatstroke and exhaustion.

But when he spoke, the voice matched the face.

Christian said, "Shut the door, would you? You're letting all the cold out."

When she didn't respond, he reached across her lap and pulled the door closed himself.

The desert raced by.

Christian reached down, grabbed a bottled water from between the seats, dropped it into her lap.

"Glad you were still here," he said. "I swapped out Isaiah's car as fast as I could, but it took longer than I'd planned."

She unscrewed the water and sucked it down.

Still cold enough to trigger a brief, blinding headache, but she didn't care. The thirst-quench was orgasmic.

"There's a whole case," he said. "Help yourself."

She killed two more, leaned back in her seat.

They were speeding along on a descending grade.

The temperature readout passing the 110 mark.

The desert looking more hostile and unforgiving with each passing mile.

Like a lifeless planet. Like that painting in Christian's office.

The hydration and the AC were going a long way toward clearing her head.

She looked over at Christian. He'd changed. Maybe others wouldn't have noticed, but to her, a student of body language, it was like riding with a completely different man. He sat straighter. His shoulders implied confidence and ability. And there was a hardness in his face that hadn't ever been there before.

He said, "Your pride is wounded. As it should be. But you should know something."

"What's that?"

"I am the very best in the world at what I do. The game was over before it ever started. It was like a middle-school kid trying to compete in the PGA Championship."

"Are you even a therapist?"

"Read a couple books. But it wouldn't be fair to say I had a practice. Or a diploma. You were my only client."

"How the hell did you do this? And *why*?"

"You first fell on my radar while you were still in prison. Friend mentioned you to me. Your work with Javier Estrada and John Fitch in the Keys was very impressive. Even then, I wanted to work with you, but I worried about your self-destructive tendencies."

Beyond the windows, the vegetation was shrinking, browning.

He said, "When you turned up in Charleston, I went to Charleston."

"But I came to you."

"Think back to how you first heard about me."

"One of the girls in the halfway house recommended you. She told me you'd changed her life. Gave me your card."

"Her name was Samantha and I paid her five thousand dollars to steer you to me."

"Jesus. You've been running this grift on me for half a year. But you helped me. You actually helped me."

"I'm glad. Although that wasn't really the purpose."

"I told you everything about me. Things nobody else knew."

"I wouldn't have had it any other way. I've never taken an interest in anyone with such intensity. I had to know you inside and out, Letty. Your secrets and fears. I needed to see your naked soul."

"It was a violation."

"Yes, but a necessary one."

"You were planning Vegas from the beginning?"

"No, that fell in my lap last month. Vegas was never the end goal."

"So what was?"

"You. Meeting you. Vetting you. Learning everything about you."

"I left Charleston and came west on my own. That was *my* decision."

"Was it really? Let's think back to the day you *decided* to leave. What happened?"

"A customer harassed me. I fought back. My boss fired me."

"Because I paid them to. I wanted you to leave town. You'd been talking about it already. You just needed a push."

"You sent me to Isaiah?"

"In a back-channel sort of way. I knew he was planning to rip me off. You might even say I was so unreasonable in my terms that I encouraged it. Isaiah's ambitious and fearless. But he's lucky I didn't leave him in the desert. I figured if he wanted to do the hard work, let him. I had Javier recommend you to him."

"So I could get on the inside and you could manipulate me."

"So I could manipulate everyone. It's what I do. I took down a casino, kept one hundred percent of the haul, and all I did was drive. And I didn't even have to do that, but I wanted to see you under pressure."

"How'd you know I'd ask you to drive us?"

"I set it up perfectly. I had helped you with your addiction. Here was a chance for you to return the favor. Give me a taste of excitement. Snap me out of my misery. Possibly save my life. Even if you hadn't called, I had alternate plans to catch up with Isaiah's crew. I'd have won no matter what you did, Letty."

"Who's the man I stole the phone from?"

"My face. I have many of them. He's probably breaking it to the crew right now that Isaiah got the better of us. And despite the fact that you tried to rip me off, you're going to get paid, Letty. Won't be seven million. But it won't be shabby."

"What'd you do to Mark?"

"He's fine. Talented kid. Maid will find him tied up in my suite tomorrow morning. We'll work together at some point in the future. As I hope you and I will. The real stars of the show," he said, "are your hands. That grab you did in the Wynn casino was in the top three I've ever seen."

"You were there?"

"I was everywhere. You're an unpolished diamond, Letty."

"Is that supposed to be a compliment?"

"Coming from me? Yes. You've got more raw talent than I've ever seen crammed into one person. But you're self-destructive."

"I'm fighting it. I'll always be fighting it. You know that."

"You're good now," he said, "but I could make you great."

The road stretched on for miles—a straight shot into hell. It dipped steadily toward a valley floor distorted by heat shimmer.

"Is that Death Valley?" she asked.

"Yep. Your purse and phone are in the backseat, by the way."

Letty glanced back, saw her belongings, and then a wall of black duffel bags stacked where the third-row seating had been removed.

"It's your pride," he said. "It's working against you right now. It's whispering, 'Who's this guy to tell me my business?'"

But he was wrong.

She said, "You couldn't be more off base."

"No?"

"I'm not perfect. But I'm woman enough to admit when I've had my ass handed to me. I am hurt, though."

"You'll get over it. There's this job," he said.

"Yeah?"

"It's a little ways off. You aren't ready yet. But you could be."

"As you know, I was on my way to Oregon when I got drawn into all this. There's nothing more important to me than seeing Jacob."

"But after that? Would you be up for some real work?"

"Vegas wasn't real enough for you?"

"My next job makes Vegas look like a child's prank. It'd be dangerous. You could lose your life. Or spend the rest of it in prison. But if there aren't stakes, what's the fun, right? Might as well rob 7-Elevens."

And if it keeps my mind off using . . .

She let her head rest against the glass. The desert heat pushing through like a plague.

Suit up and show up.

"What exactly are you proposing here?" she asked.

"I know you now, as well as you know yourself. And I might even trust you. That's all this was ever about. Let me help you take your game to the next level. Let me make you world-class."

"Are you lonely at the top? Is that it?"

"You're the first person I've met in a long time who might, someday, be able to keep up with me. Just imagine what we could accomplish together."

"I'll think about it," she said. "So is there a first name you want to let me in on? Or do you go by that iconic last?"

He didn't look over, but he smiled at the windshield as the road ahead dropped toward the lowest point in North America.

"No," he said. "When I'm with friends, all I answer to is Richter."

A NOTE FROM BLAKE CROUCH ON "GRAB"

"Grab" is perhaps the best example of how we scoured the three Letty stories that compose this volume to build our show.

The first two scenes in "Grab" feature prominently in the pilot. First, the scene in the diner when Letty gets attacked by a rapey trucker, knees him in the balls, and steals his wallet. And next, the scene of Letty in Christian's office. I actually view the absence of these two scenes in "The Pain of Others" as a knock against that story. In "The Pain of Others" we meet Letty as she's walking into the Grove Park Inn, intending to steal from the guest rooms. Chad Hodge wrote the first ten pages of the pilot script, and he made the excellent choice to use the diner/trucker scene from the first chapter of "Grab" as the opening scene of our pilot. If you think about it, it's the perfect introduction to Letty. We see her trying to hold down a lousy job. Getting shit from her boss. We see her fight back when attacked and glimpse her skill and grit as a survivor. It quickly tells us who Letty is, and (hopefully) helps us to immediately fall in love with her. If the pilot episode had begun where "The Pain of Others" starts, the audience probably wouldn't have been as sympathetic toward Letty, considering she's stealing from hotel rooms by page three.

For me, Letty's therapy scene in Christian's office is one of the great insights into her character, especially the conversation they have about the painting. I was thrilled when that scene translated almost verbatim into the television show.

The main plotline of "Grab" also plays prominently into episode five of season one, with a handful of key changes.

The main problem we had with translating "Grab" into our show was one of tone. *Always* tone. In "Grab," Letty goes to Las Vegas and gets involved in a high-stakes takedown of a casino. It involves rappelling out of a high-rise, a scene in a trendy club, and a large, highly skilled crew of criminals ripping off a casino for millions.

But the thing is, our show is lo-fi.

Our locations are predominantly diners, shitty motels, gas stations, small towns. To suddenly have Letty pulling a job in Vegas would have been a giant violation of our tone, and we definitely didn't want to see her rappelling out of a building.

So we kept the concept of Letty lifting a phone and ripping off a casino, but expressed it our way. She only steals a couple hundred thousand. She steals from dumb crooks. And the casino itself looks like nothing you'd find in Sin City. Our amazing production designer, Curt Beech, built the casino for episode five in the style of a cotton exchange, appropriate for the Savannah, Georgia, location.

Much of the Christian-Letty interactions from "Grab" and the idea that she brings him into the job fit snugly into the DNA of *Good Behavior*.

I've heard writers complain when adaptations change their work for the screen, but I don't share that hostility. I love how an idea, a character, a storyline can augment, mature, and deepen as it passes through different media.

What I like most about the process of turning a story into a visual medium is that it requires more than just me to see it through. The screenwriter Paul Schrader (*Taxi Driver*, *Raging Bull*) said, "Screenplays are invitations to others to collaborate."

And if you want to collaborate, then by definition, others are going to bring their ideas and baggage and brilliance to your work.

What started as a short story over seven years ago has become something I could never have created on my own. As much as I enjoy writing novels and stories in the quiet of my office, there's a part of my personality that thrives on creative collaboration, and my life is infinitely richer for all of the amazing actors, directors, and crew who have come together to help make this portrait of a woman named Letty Dobesh.

Dockery as Letty on the casino set, holding the stolen phone.

ACKNOWLEDGMENTS

Special thanks to . . .

My editor at Thomas & Mercer, Jacquelyn Ben-Zekry, for her brilliant editorial acumen in helping me to always bring out the best of Letty. Our first project together was "Grab" and this collaboration has been one of the most impactful in my career.

My literary agent, David Hale Smith, and the gang at InkWell Management, especially Nathaniel Jacks, Alexis Hurley, and Richard Pine.

My film and TV manager, Angela Cheng Caplan, and my entertainment attorney, Joel VanderKloot.

The team at Amazon Publishing, especially Kjersti Egerdahl, Sarah Funk, Gracie Doyle, Thom Kephart, Hai-Yen Mura, Mikyla Bruder, and Jeff Belle.

Meredith Jacobson, who did a stellar job copyediting this book.

Everyone at TNT/Turner, including Kevin Reilly, Sarah Aubrey, Sam Linsky, Adrienne O'Riain, and a special bow to Martine Resnick for her extraordinary efforts and vision to help this project land.

Becky Clements and Marty Adelstein, producing partners extraordinaire.

Our entire Wilmington, North Carolina, crew, for their tireless hours spent at night, in the rain, helping us tell this story.

Charlotte Sieling, our pilot director, who set such an amazing bar of poetic noir for all of us to strive for.

And finally, my cowriter, cocreator, copartner in crime, Chad Hodge. It has been quite the ride, my friend.

ABOUT THE AUTHOR

Blake Crouch is an internationally bestselling novelist and screenwriter. His Wayward Pines trilogy was adapted into a top-rated 2015 television series for FOX, on which M. Night Shyamalan served as executive producer. With Chad Hodge, he also created *Good Behavior*, the TNT television show starring Michelle Dockery, based on his Letty Dobesh novellas. Crouch's forthcoming novel, *Dark Matter*, has been optioned by Sony Pictures, and he is currently at work on the screenplay. Crouch has written more than a dozen novels, which have been translated into over thirty languages, and his short fiction has appeared in numerous publications, including *Ellery Queen's Mystery Magazine* and *Alfred Hitchcock's Mystery Magazine*. Crouch lives in Colorado.